I0755540

THE TWO VOCATIONS

THE TWO VOCATIONS;

OR,

THE SISTERS OF MERCY AT HOME.

A TALE.

BY THE AUTHOR OF

"THE SCHONBERG-COTTA FAMILY."

NEW YORK:
ROBERT CARTER & BROTHERS,
No. 530 Broadway.
1865.

———Thy love
Shall chant itself its own beatitudes
After its own life-working. A child's kiss
Set on thy sighing lips shall make thee glad;
A poor man, served by thee, shall make thee rich;
A sick man, helped by thee, shall make thee strong;
Thou shalt be served thyself by every sense
Of service which thou renderest

Elizabeth Barrett Browning.

Dienen lerne bei Zeiten das Weib nach ihrer Bestimmung;
Denn durch Dienen allein gelangt sie endlich zum Herrschen,
Zu der verdienten Gewalt, die doch ihr im Hause gehört.
Dienet die Schwester dem Bruder doch früh, sie dienet den Eltern,
Und ihr Leben ist immer ein ewiges Gehen und Kommen,
Oder ein Heben und Tragen, Bereiten und Schaffen für Andre.
Wohl ihr, wenn sie daran sich gewöhnt, daß kein Weg ihr zu sauer
Wird, und die Stunden der Nacht ihr sind wie die Stunden des Tages,
Daß ihr niemals die Arbeit zu klein und die Nadel zu fein dünkt,
Daß sie sich ganz vergißt und leben mag nur in Andern!

Goethe, Hermann und Dorothea.

CONTENTS.

THE TWO VOCATIONS.

I.

CHILDHOOD.

A HAPPY childhood is a rich gift and heritage from God. I think that circumstance which the biographers of St. Dominic adduce as a sign of early ripened sainthood, was in itself enough to account for all the morose asceticism of his later years, and the growth of dragons' teeth it fostered; he did not love play when he was a child, but used to steal apart from his companions to tell his beads. Narrow and dark indeed must that soul be, into which no glad light finds its way, before life with its cares and sorrows has built up and darkened its windows one by one. Heavy and sluggish indeed must that stream of life be, which gushes forth with no sweet excess of happiness, even when it flows fresh from the hand of God; which presents no joyful images to the heart, when on the dullness of after years bursts the blessed possibility of the gift of a second life—"Except ye become as a little child."

It was not so with the two lives, some of whose sources and windings in sun and shade, rough places and smooth, I happen to be acquainted with, and intend here to sketch. Love and health filled brimful the cup of childish happiness, for the cousins Annie Fielding and Kate Cameron.

The two children had wandered from the waste nook of the kitchen-garden, which was their Utopia, and were walking hand in hand, their faces full of that single-hearted earnestness which in childhood is lavished on every fleeting object, and in later life can scarcely be gathered for the highest. Catharine's elder sister Jean, their governess for the time being, was wanted at home to help entertain a deaf visitor, and so the cousins were enjoying the high festival of an extempore half-holiday, the treasure of a whole afternoon to do what they liked with. Such a piece of good fortune might be expected to awaken ambitious projects; and it did. The children had issued from the charmed circle of Eastwood, Catharine's home, and were on their way along the high road to Mr. Cameron's counting-house to present a petition in due form, deeming that so important a request must warrant even so daring an intrusion.

They had started on their adventure with a courage and heroism worthy of success. That reach of the turnpike-road was to them a kind of high seas, only to be traversed under the convoy of Nurse or Jean; and the glass manufactory which was the scene of Mr. Cameron's daily labor, with its offices and courts and furnaces, and hot, blackened workmen, rushing to and fro, a mysterious territory, as little to be entered on without a guide as any circle of Dante's Inferno; but the greater the daring the greater the joy. Nevertheless their hearts grew gradually less and less confident as the half-mile which intervened between the manufactory and the garden-gate diminished beneath their busy little feet, and their pace unconsciously slackened. Then it had to be debated who was to be the Mercury. Catharine wished to lay the burden on Annie, because she so seldom asked for anything and was such a pet of Mr. Cameron's, and Catharine being usually the commander by the "divine right" of being able and willing to command, Annie tremblingly assented, and a little speech was concocted which she solemnly promised to deliver.

But at the very goal a new difficulty awaited them. There were two gentlemen in Mr. Cameron's office, (one Kate remembered afterwards was called Miller,)—and Mr. Cameron had his most furrowed business face on,

THE COUSINS AT THE MANUFACTORY.

Two Vocations. p. 4.

so that when the children had watched them out, from the corner in which they had ensconced themselves behind a friendly screen, fright and suspense had entirely driven the speech out of Annie's mind.

Fortunately, however, Mr. Cameron caught a glimpse of her before she could speak, and like the great Gustavus on a similar occasion, he spared the child all further difficulties by coming forward and catching her in his arms. Then seating her on the desk, and holding her hands in one of his whilst with the other arm he planted Catharine on his knee, he said—

"Now, young women, what penalty must I inflict on you for this offence—vagrancy and house-breaking? I must look through my great law-books to see."

"Oh, papa, we deserve nothing of the kind; it is only a petition," exclaimed Catharine, Annie meanwhile sitting crimson and quiet.

"What, begging too!—Worse and worse!"

1*

"Dear papa, it is only something nobody cares for, that belongs to nobody; we want you—we want you to give us the island at the bottom of the kitchen-garden."

"A very modest request truly, Kate! why with an island at ten, you will want a continent at twenty."

"Oh no, papa, a continent would not do at all; we want it for a particular purpose."

"Indeed! And on what terms do you propose becoming my tenants, annual or on lease? or would you prefer the fee-simple? I do not know but that might give you a vote for the next election."

"Papa, papa, you will not be serious; we want it—for a Robinson Crusoe's island."

Annie looked alarmed at this revelation, but Kate continued eagerly—

"Oh you *will* let us have it, dear papa; you know we are not often beggars, and if you will only give us this, we will never want anything more."

Mr. Cameron's face changed from its seriocomic expression to one of gentle tenderness as he stroked back his little girl's wild hair. Kate continued, eagerly interpreting his silence into acquiescence, but Annie, raising her large grey eyes, and fixing them for a moment doubtfully on her uncle's, dropt them again, and said, coloring still deeper—

"Dear uncle Cameron, do not give it us if you think it would not be good. We will try to do without."

Kate turned round suddenly with flashing eyes, and frowned most ominously at Annie, murmuring, "Of course papa knows that, Annie." Then she continued, "Indeed she wishes for it quite as much as I do, papa—indeed we both so set our hearts on it."

"Indeed I think she does, Kate," said Mr. Cameron. Kissing them, and then setting them on the floor, he added, "There, go now—I am busy, go and ask mamma and Jean."

"Jean does not know anything about it," replied Catharine; "but may we tell mamma you do not object?"

"You may tell mamma; if she is not afraid to trust you on a desert island—I am not."

Full of joyous eagerness, the little girls danced out of the office, Kate insisting on construing this commission into a deed of gift, and indignantly controverting all Annie's conscientious scruples on the subject.

When they reached the house, the hall was cleared in a moment, and the drawing-room door opened, and Catharine's hands were gently stretched over her mother's shoulders so as to hide the book she was reading; and speaking very fast and almost in a whisper, between want of breath and her desire to be very gentle, she said—

"One moment, dear mamma—papa has consented; we may have the island, may we not?"

"My dear child, how flushed you are! what have you been doing?" exclaimed Mrs. Cameron in a tone of languid surprise.

"Will you stand still for a moment, Kate?"

said Jean, quietly, as she collected the scattered contents of her work-basket, which Kate had upset in her progress; "you have caught your foot in one of my balls of Berlin wool." And so poor Kate had to experience the chill of addressing an audience, by no means wound up to her own pitch of enthusiasm, and to undertake the difficult task of explaining and pleading for a thing which to her was beyond all proof.

"What island does she mean, Jean?" said Mrs. Cameron at length.

"The waste bit, by the deep pool, I suppose," replied Jean, "out of which Nero dragged Kate last midsummer twelvemonths."

"What madness! My dear child, I should never have a moment's peace of mind when you were out of my sight."

"How could you say anything so extremely unjust and unkind, Jean?" exclaimed Kate, all her eagerness foaming into indignation against this unexpected obstacle. "That is not at all what I mean; besides I was almost a baby then, and I am two years older now, and I should never go there without Annie."

Jean's calm handsome face changed not, and she made no retort..

"But why do you want it?" said Mrs. Cameron, half-relenting, as she saw Kate's cheeks crimsoning, and the tears gathering rapidly in her eyes; "why will not the kitchen-garden do as well?"

"Because, because," said Kate, with a quivering voice, "it is not an island, and we want to be Robinson Crusoes. It is Annie's idea," she continued, appealing to her cousin, who blushed, but did not deny the authorship.

"But cannot you be Robinson Crusoes in the kitchen-garden, where there would be no chance of your getting drowned?"

Kate very nearly cried with the bathos of the thought. "Oh dear mamma, how could we? there is no hollow tree for a cave, and no beach for the savages; besides, Nero would never stay in that corner, and he is to be our lama."

Mrs. Cameron could not help smiling at this array of unconquerable arguments, and Kate was eagerly pressing her advantage, when the door softly opened and in glided a little lady in black, almost old enough, and brisk enough, and tiny enough, to represent the good fairy which in Kate's eyes she at that moment was.

"Oh Grannie, Grannie, you are sure to be on our side!" she exclaimed, seizing one of her hands, whilst Annie gently disengaged the umbrella and work-basket from the other.

The little lady seemed by no means aggrieved at these somewhat overpowering attentions, but suffered herself to be led to Mrs. Cameron's judgment-seat, where she was welcomed with a greeting as cordial as that of the children. And so it was at length decided that Grannie was to accompany the children to the disputed territory, and on her report sentence was to be given.

Forth, therefore, the trio sallied, Kate escorting the umbrella, and Annie retaining possession of the work-basket, while both held one of the old lady's hands; and as they went every little plan and project was unfolded eagerly to their visitor, every little plan that Jean would have deemed too childish for a moment's notice, and even Mrs. Cameron might have grown weary of. But Grannie never tired. Her heart, "at leisure from itself," and unburdened by the thousand petty cares which wrinkle and cripple it far more than sorrow, was, when not possessed by some earnest work, as lightly borne on any chance breeze as a child's. And never was the laugh merrier or the game more eager than when Grannie joined in it. The gaiety of childhood infected her, and the sunshine of her loving nature dispersed every cloud that might have gathered into a storm.

They went across the lawn, and down the steep side-path of the kitchen-garden, terraced like the vineyards of the Côte d'or, and lying like them on the sunny southward slope of the valley; the opposite side being less steep, and the wood which clothed it bordered by a broad green meadow. The gooseberry-bushes were beginning to show a faint tinge of green; the old wall at the top, against which the best fruit-trees were nailed, began to glisten with white and pink blossoms; even the old forked apple-tree, in the corner, was preparing to array itself for its summer-work of sheltering Kate and Annie, as they sate amongst its knotted branches, and read of giant-land, or elfin-land, or of old heroic days, eating sour apples at intervals. Below the kitchen-garden was a cherry-orchard, and below the cherry-orchard was a green path, skirting the river, which just there was still and deep enough to inspire confidence in rushes and large-leaved water-plants to make incursions on its bed, and to invite the self-complacent gaze of many alders and willows. That evening the shadows of the rocks lay calmly and solemnly across it. But a moment after its character entirely changed, and the quiet brown waters were hurried over the weir. For an instant they seemed to fall smoothly and heavily, as if they could not help it; but then all at once, entering into the fun, they treated the affair as if it were their own choice, and leapt from rock to rock in cascades of amber, and agate, and pearl, keeping up the joke a long way on, whirling, and eddying, and foaming around every stone and pebble, and making the quiet valley ring with their shouts and peals of laughter, now loud and boisterous as a schoolboy's, and anon silvery and musical as a fairy's.

And for hundreds of years it had been the same, the brown waters had moved demure and unsuspecting to the brink, were precipitated in startled helplessness over it, and then seizing the spirit of the thing, dashed along in the wildest merriment. And the willows were as imperturbable, and the burst of sudden mirth as fresh, and the echoes of the valley as surprised and noisy, as ever. And the little green island, which divided the waters just below, nestled as quietly in their laughing embrace, only now and then shaking the spray from the long green ringlets of its willows, which were rather ladylike and particular. But the forget-me-nots and the old gnarled oak, on the mossy rock in the middle, enjoyed it to their hearts' content, and grew the bluest forget-me-nots and the most stalwart old oak in all the country round.

All this Grannie saw, and the beauty and life of the scene sent a glow into her heart; but Kate and Annie saw only (what was quite as beautiful in their eyes) a shallow ford, narrow enough for Grannie to cross with the aid of some slippery moss-grown rocks, but also sufficiently difficult to guard their paradise from vulgar steps; a hollow trunk for a cave, a little grassy plot for a farm, and some dry rocks, which might be built into a granary; so true is it, that whilst to some Nature is

—die hohe, die himmlische Göttin, dem andern

she is

Eine tüchtige Kuh, die sie mit Butter versorgt.*

How much of the fresh beauty of the place may, nevertheless, have found its way unconsciously into their hearts, and given color and music to thoughts, and visions of after years, I cannot pretend to say.

"Who knows the individual hour in which
His habits were first sown, even as a seed?
Who that shall point as with a wand, and say,
This portion of the river of my mind
Came from that fountain?"

Yet I doubt not that these unconscious creatures minister in a thousand mute and unsuspected ways to that conscious and immortal spirit, which God has given them for awhile to tend and care for Him, even as the wild wolves of the old Roman legend nursed

* The high and heavenly goddess, to others
She is as the useful milch-cow, which provides them with butter.

the forsaken children of the king; often bewildered by the strange freaks of the foster-child; whom with blind, loving instincts, they are training for a destiny, and a home, of which neither nurse nor nursling can conceive. Certainly, such scenes do imprint an additional strength and tenderness on the memories of days and companions passed away.

"See, dear Grannie," said the children, speaking in rapid responses, or oftener both at once, Annie's shyness being quite overwhelmed by the eager joy of the new plan, "here against this dry rock we intend to plant somes stakes, and roof them with straw, to garner up the fallen fruit, which is our perquisite; and here we intend to dig some steps to the water; this is the beach where we intend to light our fire—only," added Kate, observing the doubtful effect of this last announcement, "*only a very dull fire*, to roast potatoes. And gardener has promised us some potatoes, and to carve us some seats,

—if Kenneth does not come home in time. And by-and-by, in the summer holidays,—may I tell, Annie?—we must tell Grannie,—we mean to get Cook to lend us an old kettle, and to ask mamma, and papa, and Jean, and aunt and uncle Fielding, and you to tea."

"In what character are we to appear?" said Grannie; "as savages?"

"We had not thought of that," said Kate, appealing in some perplexity to Annie; "but you know, Grannie, that will not be play, the tea will be in earnest."

So between the "tea in earnest," and the other undeniable qualifications of the plan, Grannie professed herself won over.

Then as they returned up the garden, rather a toilsome and breathless ascent for Grannie, Annie gently pushing, and Kate flattering herself she was supporting her on her little round arm,—at each pause the old lady had some pleasant word to say, or some pleasant thing to point out, until at length they persuaded her to rest awhile on the seat in the recess under the sunny wall which bounded the highest terrace. The sun was just sending up a glowing smile on the blossoms he had opened, from the low place in the sky to which he had sunk, on his way behind the distant hills, and they sate there until the last twinkling crimson point of light had vanished, and the golden flood had changed to silver, and the cold winds, and the stars came out one by one from under the shadow of night.

But who can tell the many sweet and solemn words Grannie said to the children in that quiet hour—words they could no more recall than the shapes and lines of the clouds which faded as they looked and listened, but which left around the garden-seat a holy spell, and linked the sunset and the clouds for them with brighter things beyond, and God!

"Annie," said Kate that night when she went up with her cousin to put on her things, —Kate had been unwontedly quiet all the evening,—"Annie, I have a plan!—We will plant the garden with flax, to make clothes for the little heathen girls Grannie was telling us of."

Annie thought it would be beautiful, if they could only learn to spin.

And how much further this project might have been developed it is impossible to say, had not Mr. Cameron's cheerful voice sounded up the stairs, "Children, children, what are you about? you will meet again to-morrow."

So the parting came at last—last words forgotten till that moment; important commissions that could not be remembered; "good-nights," as much in danger as any of Romeo's of being prolonged "until it were to-morrow,"—reluctant, backward glances, fervent kisses; then the emptiness of the house, when Annie was fairly gone, nothing but sleep henceforward to hope for! The half-holiday was indeed over!

II.

INTRODUCTIONS.

And now whilst Kate is quiet, that is to say, asleep, let me introduce you a little more at length to the various members of the family group, into which we have so unceremoniously intruded.

Grannie, in spite of her matronly title, had never been married. In days long past, when Mrs. Cameron was Catharine Fielding, a pretty orphan girl left in reduced circumstances, with one wild elder brother, and a little sister who died young, and was enshrined in the memory of the children as the child aunt, who would never grow old, Grannie, then although no longer young, the youngest of a large family living in opulence, had persuaded her father, Mr. Davison, to let her adopt the little Kate of those days. And so the child became to Margaret Davison as a daughter, and to the rest of the family a little caressed pet.

Margaret had early learned the sinfulness and weakness of her own nature, and the solemn responsibilities of life, and had early sought and found that faith which unites the heart in loving relationship to God; and the orphan was to her no mere plaything, but a precious deposit lent her by God, to train for Him, loved (if ever any but a mother could so love) with all the tenderness and watchful solicitude of a mother's love. And her care was blessed. Although the child's character was not naturally of the stature or strength of Margaret's, it had features of its own which were very fascinating and loveable; and so, when she had reached the age of twenty, thought Mr. Cameron.

At first Margaret rather resented any one's laying claim to the first place in her child's affections, and was disposed to think

Catharine not a little fickle and ungrateful for seeming inclined to accord it to him—perhaps the only instance in which her love showed itself a little less unselfish than that of a mother. For twelve years she had watched the child with the tenderest care, risked infection in nursing her through childish sicknesses, bent the whole energy of her mind to develop hers, lavished the whole treasure of her love upon her; and now another was to enter into her labors. Besides, there were chambers opened by this, which were to Margaret as chambers of mourning, ever dark and closed. But this feeling of jealousy was very transient, and never such as to cast an hour's shade on Catharine's happiness. Even in her first surprise she pleaded for a marriage-portion for the culprit, and very soon she learned that the enlarging of Catharine's world was also the discovery of a new world to her—that the heart is not a *treasury* which is impoverished by giving, but a *power* which is strengthened and enriched by loving; that

Catharine could indeed love all better for loving one beyond all.

So Catharine was married, and Margaret Davison became more decidedly the old maid. Then sorrow came to her; her family were scattered one by one, and some died, and at length the feeble hand which still held the broken links together, relaxed its hold, and the whole fell asunder.

After her father's death, on looking into his affairs, it was found that he had overestimated his property, and the handsome provision he had assigned her, could not be secured to her without injuring the other children. Margaret at once relinquished her claim, and the two brothers, on whom the cares of this world had wrought their usual drying and hardening effects, when no heavenly dews are suffered to counteract the "heat of the day," and no heavenly Friend is sought on whom to cast its burdens,—consoled themselves with thinking that it could not matter much to Margaret, as she had no family to provide for, and with allowing her two hundred a year.

And if you had seen Margaret Davison in her little abode, you might have deemed them right. What, indeed, could she want more than she had, as she often said to herself, when she drew her easy-chair to the fire, and the faithful old servant who would not leave her in her low estate, brought in the kettle and the cozy tea-tray, and she set her feet on a brioche of Catharine's knitting,—or in the summer looked beyond the triangular patch of garden to the hills, whilst on the table was a fresh nosegay of wild flowers which little loving hands had gathered. She never numbered the loss of wealth among her trials, except in the one point of the loss of the luxury of giving. Other trials she had had, early ones, still scarcely to be spoken of, casting their shadow on this her sunny eventide of life; but what heart in all the family of God was ever moulded without them? what stone ever fitted for the heavenly temple without some rough blows? And for the little sorrows and aches and cares which still occasionally sprang up to trouble her, she used to say they were only the delicate touches of the chisel, and bow herself patiently to them, never being left unsupported by the tenderest as well as the strongest of all Comforters. Then Catharine's children, Jean, and Kenneth, and Kate, and the little Annie, —what new vistas of life they opened for her, what new well-springs of love, almost making this old world too fresh and dear!

And while we speak of her as old, and cannot assign to her any age much below sixty, none of those who knew her ever thought of her as the elderly lady, and to the children, not even the child-aunt, whom God had made an angel, could have a fresher glow of youth about her. She was their counsellor and comforter, the playmate with whom they never quarrelled, the story-book which never tired; not that Grannie dealt in fiction, but what fairy tale, German or Arabian, could be so wonderful and real as histories of what mamma did when she was a little girl, or the still remoter antiquity of Grannie's own childhood, with its strange historical customs and costumes? And then there were Sunday stories, dearer and more treasured than any, listened to with earnest upturned faces, and cheeks often wet with silent tears, and holy evening hours linked with Grannie, whilst Mrs. Cameron was resting on the sofa, or discussing weighty economical questions with her husband,—for we have to do with what was, not what might have been; and Mrs. Cameron's character, although very motherly and tender, was such as to bind her children's hearts to her rather by passive amiability and sweetness and need of care, than by any very active exertions in their behalf, self-denial not entering very largely into her catalogue of Christian virtues, although loving-kindness did.

Jean had never been thrown so much under Grannie's influence as Kate and Annie.

She was seven years older than Kate, and had had a governess, and altogether a very complete education, being possessed of many more languages and accomplishments than she knew what to do with; and since she had left the school-room in the capacity of pupil, she had re-entered it as supreme governess and instructress of her sister and cousin. A neat, quiet, orderly being, in every respect so unruffled and orthodox, from her hair to her opinions, Jean never did or thought anything irregular; everything she undertook she accomplished, and accomplished neatly and well, from the first little cap she plaited for her doll, to the Essay on the Sublime and Beautiful, which with the large head of Minerva over the school-room mantelpiece, were the crowning-points of her scholastic attainments. Her person was a type of her inner life: of middle height, graceful, perhaps a little too erect, with a placid brow, Grecian, neither high nor low, pale and fair, with large light quiet eyes, and a mouth in which sweetness was saved from insipidity by the pride of the short upper lip. She seemed as if she must have entered the world full-grown and full-dressed like the fairy-wife, who sprang out of the walnut-shell, for the favored prince. And it had always been the same, a point of history which Kate knew to her cost, meeting her as it did like a warning spectre at every turn of her erratic course. In the nursery it was—

"If you could only have seen the order in which Miss Jean used to keep her drawers and her baby-house,"—and the melancholy contrast between the hairless dolls, and headless horses, and voiceless cats of her own babyhood, and the inheritance of unbroken toys which had descended to her.

In the drawing-room,—"I must really dress you in sackcloth, Kate. I cannot think how it is, Jean never tore her things in this way." Or, "When will your shoulders be as straight as Jean's?"

In the school-room, the very walls hung

with silent reproaches in the shape of drawings finished by Jean at an age when Kate could draw nothing but Chinese illustrations to her own fictions, on the slate.

There could not be a greater contrast, or a greater enigma, than the two sisters were to each other. Jean's habitual conviction was, that Kate was a particularly naughty child, whilst Kate wavered between deeming Jean the most precise and tiresome person in the world, and an ideal of unattainable perfection; which latter idea commonly succeeded a fit of fiercest rebellion, and was expressed in innumerable passionate bursts of repentance, and occasionally in penitential letters, accompanied with presents of some cherished childish treasure, which Jean received with a gracious but desponding act of amnesty. Grannie's private opinion was, nevertheless, that Kate's mind was of richer soil than Jean's. The seeds of knowledge lay safe in Jean's mind as in the little pasteboard boxes she made for her garden-seeds;

not one was lost, but not one germinated: or, like the laburnam seeds children string into necklaces, they made ornaments for her person;—but in Kate's mind they became living things; and whilst a hundred, perhaps, perished and were lost, here and there one sprang up and blossomed, and again bore seed-vessels, whose future multiplication no one could limit, nor what store of seed to the sower or bread to the eater of after years they might yield. Kate could scarcely repeat correctly a summary of any chapter of history, but of her favorite events, or heroes, she could tell you the minutest particulars. Grannie thought she saw in the two sisters the difference between mechanism and life; but whatever she thought she kept to herself, and whilst she often pleaded with Jean for Kate, she oftener exhorted Kate herself, and Grannie's exhortations were generally effectual; for, unlike Jean's, they were founded on hope.

With Annie Fielding it was quite different.

Had it not been for Kate, I suppose she never would have been in a scrape in her life. Less impetuous and daring, at least in action, she resembled her aunt Cameron more than any of her own children; but she resembled still more her own father, who, after a somewhat wild youth, had subsided, rather than risen, into a sober clergyman of the neighboring country-town of Milbourne,—evangelical in sentiment, but rather in sentiment than in principle; full of intellectual dreams and useful schemes, which, but for his Annie's stepmother, his second wife, and in all possible respects his curate, would never have been carried out. She was an energetic woman, who found in six children, and a parish, with clothing societies, working societies, district societies, schools, and workhouse, small scope for her superabundant energies, and therefore undertook the management of her husband and the curates *par parenthese.* Annie was the only child of her father's first marriage, and was gladly permitted to spend the greater portion of her time at Eastwood. The cast of her character was more intellectual than her cousin's, although she was thought less clever, and looked up to Kate's clear, rapid mind, with contented reverence. Or rather, in the command which Kate naturally assumed, and Annie naturally conceded, in all their affairs, might be seen the preponderance of character over mere intellect. Kate exercised over Annie a masculine control, guiding her actions; Annie, in later years, a feminine influence over Kate, unconsciously moulding her opinions. Annie schemed, and Kate executed. Annie would pause over a beautiful thought or picture; Kate would be hurried away by enthusiasm for a noble action. Kate's visions were of old Spartan heroes, or of the Scottish chieftains, whose blood it was her joy to think flowed in her veins; whilst Annie dreamt of Undines, and angelic beings, water-spirits, air-spirits, and fire-spirits, and would enchain Kate by dreamy narrations of the elves of the hills and the river, their beauty, their sorrows and joys, and the marvellous glory of the palaces where they lived; being liable, however, to sudden interruptions from Kate just when her own fancy was most enrapt. Kate's ideals were all chivalrous, only *she* must be the adventurous knight, and not the passive rescued damosel; Annie's day-dreams were of fairy-land, or of quiet, tender homes.

Annie had, perhaps, altogether more of innate taste and artist's love of beauty for its own sake than Kate, as was illustrated by the gloss of her luxuriant hair, and the unconscious grace of her slight childish figure, and the dress, which, if sometimes disordered, was never slovenly, in contrast with Kate's elf-locks, which never would retain the combs, and shoulders, which never could be kept within the frock, and the various small awkwardnesses which were to her the fruitful source of so many childish miseries.

III.

THE HOME.

THE pedigree of Eastwood House was not very distinguished. Whilst with its Doric portico and large modern windows, opening by stone steps on the lawn, it presented (as the auction bills say) an imposing front, the back-rooms bore plain testimony to their humble origin, the principal apartments of an old-fashioned farmhouse, whether, in this world of vicissitude, itself a degraded manorial residence, I cannot say.

The school-room, where the cousins spent so many of their busy hours, had been in olden times that unfrequented sanctuary, the farmhouse parlor; and, in spite of the low ceiling, with its whitewashed rafters still further lowering it, it was a cheerful room.

The windows were low and broad, with a high window-seat, and stone mullions, and diamond-paned casements, which it was Kate's first morning care to open, in order to air her little nursery of a monthly rose, a dwarf fuschia, and a Chinese primrose. One window looked on a poultry-yard, which, with its perpetual little domestic dramas, engrossed a large share of the children's attention; the other, into which roses and honeysuckles peeped on summer-days, opened on the lawn sloping gently to the river, which had there subsided into a quiet and highly respectable river, setting an edifying example of being seen and not heard.

Over the chimney-piece (a chimney-piece by courtesy, inasmuch as it offered very insufficient standing-room to the earthenware shepherds, and stags, and cats, which had been Nurse's memorials of Kate's birthdays) was a sallow-complexioned mirror, framed in black, and set there apparently to enforce any moral lessons against vanity. Opposite the poultry-yard was a grand piano, which had seen better days; and between the windows was the *chiffonniere*, with its cupboard for lesson-books, and its upper shelves filled with Kate's own books, and a few precious stray ones of her mother's, written before story-books were taught to spin lessons, and an incipient mineralogical cabinet not very scientifically arranged. These, with a large box-ottoman, degraded to a toy-warehouse, the usual odds and ends of chairs and tables, which find their way into the room in the house lowest in the social scale, constituted the furniture of the school-room, which, out of school hours, was the children's own territory.

Jean sat by the window sewing, a sunbeam resting on her simply-parted hair, and on her fair dropt eyelids; Annie was copying Attention, from Le Brun's Passions; and Kate endeavoring to illustrate the emotion in a second repetition of a list of very hard dates. She looked at Jean, and up at the mirror, and down at Annie, and then resolutely at vacancy, until at length, with some mistakes and some timely suggestions from Jean, the lesson was finished, and with the triumphant announcement, Cæsar invades Britain, B.C. 55, the book was closed, Jean left the room, and the children had the precious hour before dinner to themselves.

Why was it that the whole energy of their minds could be given to their own childish schemes, and pains and thought lavished upon these which would have ground twice the requisite quantity of lessons? It was partly, doubtless, from the preference of our poor distorted natures to do what no "ought" binds us to, but it was also partly Jean's fault. The most common, and yet the loftiest office of woman, except perhaps the office of the comforter—that of education, was to her a mechanical toil. She used her brushes more like a house-painter engaged at so much a yard, than an artist whose heart is in his subject. She went to her work too much as to a task, too much as to something to be patiently endured than something to be cheerfully done. A certain quantity of information and skill had been deposited in her mind, as water is pumped into a stone fountain, and there it lay, ready to make jets for fête-days, or to remain quiescent until sought,—and she was now ready to render a similar service to her sister, and was sorely perplexed at the porous nature of the material, baffling her persevering efforts; but of knowledge, as a living spring flowing fresh through natural channels, itself scarcely seen but in the life and freshness which spring up in its course,—of the awakening and strengthening of the mind itself, Jean had little idea. Thus, as is perhaps the case with most of us, the accidental education of the cousins was far more productive than their systematic instruction, and the travels and biographies, and even the fairy tales and childish stories which they devoured so eagerly on rainy days on the school-room window-seat, economising the last gleam of light, and in fine weather on the apple-tree, or the island, were gradually peopling their world with gentle, and brave, and heroic names,—no voiceless shadows to the loving heart and vivid imagination of childhood,—and with a rich scenery of thoughts and things.

But Jean was not satisfied. She had been pained the day before by the preference shown by the children to Grannie over herself; and although no one could be jealous of Grannie, and Jean was at once too generous and too quiescent to be troubled by any such passion, that evening, in the quiet of her own room, she endeavored to examine herself candidly as to the cause. She feared something was failing in her management,—she could not reproach herself with any one omission, or even with ever yielding to irritability, much as she was often tried,—but she still was conscious of something grating and out of tune; and the result of her earnest meditations was, that she resolved the next morning to go and consult Grannie. Accordingly, just as Grannie had finished her dinner the next day, a tap was heard at the door sufficiently gentle to indicate that it was not Kate.

Grannie wondered a little at this visit, Jean's day being in general too regularly mapped out for her to have any spare corners for extempore morning-calls—and at first she feared something was the matter at Eastwood. All her questions on this point having been answered satisfactorily, there was a pause—Grannie poked the fire, set on fresh coals, took up her knitting, and seated herself again, but the silence still continuing, she laid her knitting-needles on her knee, lowered her spectacles, and looked inquiringly over them at Jean.

"Is anything the matter, Jean?"

"Nothing, dear Grannie," said Jean, hesitating, "but the old complaint. It is a great distress to me that the children do not get on better or enjoy their lessons more, and last night I was wondering if the fault might be, after all, in me. I am sure," she continued, "I try to do my best, but Kate does not improve as I feel she might, and Annie, although she is very gentle and good, seems quite rejoiced when the lessons are over."

"Children will love play, my dear," was the reply; "and they are not weakened, but refreshed, by it."

"But they are never fresh for school, Grannie. I am sure something must be wrong."

"Can you think of nothing you might remedy?"

"Nothing," she replied rather bitterly, "except that I am afraid I have not the faculty of teaching. I was thinking this morning I would ask mamma to get a governess." Grannie laid down her work, and crossing to Jean's side of the fire, laid her hand on hers.

"Dear Jean," she said, "the woods would be very silent if no bird sang but those that sing best."

"But people have different gifts."

"Undoubtedly: but all have gift enough to do their duty. You have not sought this work, my child, it lies in your path, and what we must seek to meet such daily work is not gifts but graces."

"Oh, Grannie," said Jean very softly, tears filling her eyes, "do you think I do not pray?"

It was an effort to Jean to break so far through her natural reserve, and Grannie appreciated it.

"What do you pray for?" she said. Jean was silent. "You pray for strength to do your duty; do you pray for a heart to love it?"

"How is it possible, Grannie? If you only knew how trying it is. But the children love you."

"And why do they not love you, Jean?"

"I don't know;—perhaps because I am quiet and reserved. I suppose," she added, the tears fairly falling, "I am not suited to children."

"Nonsense, my child," said Grannie; "does not the Artist know best how to choose His pencils, and are not you *given* this subject by Him?" Then she added earnestly, "Jean, you are conscious of a blessed relationship to God. You have recognised His Son as your Saviour. You look up to Him as a forgiven child. What made you first love Him?"

"We love Him because He first loved us," said Jean.

"Then why not try to win Kate and Annie's love in the same way? Why should not the feeling between you be, instead of a mutual endurance of one another's faults, a mutual sisterly love and delight in one another's gifts? Alas, let not that melancholy word, which has become so common in the Christian Church, be introduced into Christian families! Do not let toleration take the place of love. Think, dear Jean, what a trust is committed to you, how solemn and how happy—to place tools in those little hands from which so much may be moulded—to write words on those childish hearts which may shine in illuminated letters to God's glory for ever.—Christ's work, Jean, which He paused in the midst of His most solemn teaching to bless, can you not love it?"

Jean paused, and then said—

"But, dear Grannie, we cannot love all we have to do,—and surely the sacrifice is not the less acceptable because it costs us something."

"Certainly, many mechanical tasks are to be done in this world which we cannot love; but teaching is not a mechanical task,—it is to the Christian a work of the ministry, and all such direct services must, I believe, to be effectual, be labors of love."

"Of love to His name?" said Jean inquiringly.

"That, indeed, is the spring of all," said Grannie. "Delight in duty first as His will, and you will soon delight in it for its own sake. Pray for more love, Jean; none ever taught successfully without loving the pupils and the labor. I believe God would have His servants, from angels downwards, *sing* at their work. It is we who, in our ignorant asceticism, set the needle to bore iron, and the sculptor's chisel to square paving-stones, and the pickaxe to polish gems, and then wonder that the needle breaks, and the chisel is blunted, and the gems are spoiled. I believe the Great Task-master commonly sets His servants about work they love, because the work we love is the work we are made for. And one thing more," she added, as Jean rose to leave the room,—"you pray; expect your prayers to be answered. Work in love, and work also in hope. Believe that in due season you shall reap; believe that Kate and Annie will be better through life for the toil and thought you spend on them, and I am sure they will."

Jean returned home. She had many struggles with her own pride. Was not Grannie harsh and unjust to her? What had she left undone, what unkindness had she ever been guilty of? Was not her mother satisfied? But Jean's conscience was not satisfied,—she was honest and patient, and having once found the end of the tangled skein, she would not let it go, whatever knots and mazes she might have to encounter, before she had unravelled it. On viewing everything in the light of a Higher Will, and a more loving Heart than her own, and remembering how faith in the message of His infinite love had once set her heart free, its burdens were lifted off again; and she felt that if she had not done little, she had not loved much—and her whole nature growing warm and expanding in the sunshine of that Presence, she planned and purposed many things, and, amongst others, that she would devote a regular time daily to affectionate prayer for her pupils. But this passed in secret, and all that Kate and Annie saw was, that when Jean came into the school-room the next day, her face was brightened out of its usual quiet day-light into positive sunlight, and that she kissed them very kindly, and said—

"Dear Kate and Annie, before we begin our lessons, let us kneel down and ask God to bless us in them; for you know we can do nothing without His help." It was a great effort to Jean to say this. Kate was not sure that she liked it, but certain it was, that that morning the usual chapter in the Bible was read with quite a different feeling, the geography seemed interesting, and even the sums consented to be proved.

"How kind Jean was this morning!" said Kate, musingly, at the play-hour; and even on Crusoe's island they could speak of nothing else.

"I always loved cousin Jean," said Annie,

"but I never knew before that she loved me."

But Kate's surprise was brought to a climax the next morning, by finding, when she came to open the casement for her beloved plants, that they had grown in the night to four, by the addition of a geranium which she recognised as a favorite of Jean's.

To be at Jean's door, in Jean's room, sobbing around Jean's neck, was the work of a moment.

"O Jean, I have been the naughtiest child in the world. I shall never forgive myself."

"We will forgive each other, dear Kate," said Jean gently, "and love each other, will we not?" And Jean forgot to say a word of remonstrance in favor of her disarranged hair, although it took her ten minutes to set it right again.

But I must not linger longer over the childhood of my heroines. Time would fail me to tell how many metamorphoses the island underwent, from Crusoe's island to

Britain invaded by the Romans—to the Retreat of Polish Exiles in Siberia—to the Home of Undine—to a wheat-field for the Missionaries,—or how knowledge gradually grew precious to the children, and one day they were seized with a longing to learn German, and Jean demurred, seeing they could not yet speak very good French, and Grannie opined that voluntary labor might sweeten involuntary, and Mrs. Cameron bought books and engaged a meek little German lady from the neighboring town of Milbourne;—or how once they wandered up the valley alone, amongst the gray granite rocks and the wild things that grew among them, with a delicious sense of freedom and daring, tempered in Annie by sundry scruples and fears, and did not reach home till dark, and were cried over, and kissed, and scolded, and sent to bed; or how Kenneth came back at intervals from the great public school, and laughed at their plays and projects, and made them bridges and uncouth chairs and boxes, and entertained them with marvellous tales of school-boy daring, until in Annie's eyes he grew into a Roland the Brave, and the school into an Universe; and Kate, with a mixture of mortification and reverence, felt how small their plans and adventures were, and how very little and childish she was,—and longed to be a boy.

One day more I may bring out, one of those days which shine out from the bright but confused memories of childhood, like a distant field amongst the hills on which a sunbeam rests escaping through an April shower, and makes it green as the fresh grass at our feet, yet radiant as with a light from fairy-land.

It was Sunday, and a summer-day. Kate had indulged in a fit of rebellion at the beginning of the week, and, as usual after such outbreaks, the subsequent days had been spent in a most exemplary manner. Mrs. Cameron had spoken to her very seriously, and the mother's admonitions, rare and gentle as they were, had always an irresistible power over Kate's feelings. And afterwards her uncle Fielding had preached a sermon on the free and urgent invitations to all who thirsted to come to the living waters, to come in poverty and yet in confidence. Kate had felt it extremely, and altogether her heart was quite softened. In the afternoon, locking herself into her own little room, she had prayed, and wept, and read the promises in the Bible with great joy, and had risen with a determination never to be naughty any more; and, just as she was finishing, Nurse came to the door, and in a hurry and confusion she put away her Bible and ran to open it—and communicated her resolution with many protestations to Nurse.

Nurse looked rather doubtful, and received the announcement with provoking coolness—"Well, Miss Kate, I am sure that is good news—but we shall see."

Kate was rather inclined to lose her temper at such unmerited scepticism, but she consoled herself with thinking that Nurse did not know how different this resolution was from any other; and proceeding quietly to Mrs. Cameron's room, knocked very gently at the door. "Dear mamma," she said, throwing her arms round her neck, "I hope now I shall be quite a different child always, and never trouble you any more. I have asked God to help me."

Mrs. Cameron's eyes filled with tears, half of pleasure and half of pity, and she took the child on her knee and talked sweetly and encouragingly to her. Then Grannie came, and they obtained permission to go and visit a little crippled child she had often spoken of; and leaving the fields and gardens lying in their Eden rest, they penetrated into a little dark by-street of the town, and there, above a room where the rest of the family were talking and smoking, the poor woman led Grannie and Kate to the bed-room, well-peopled with beds, where on a low crib in the corner lay a little emaciated child. Her large eyes looked restlessly out from the sunken cheeks, with that expression of old anxiety so unnatural and painful in infancy, as if the dumb soul within were wistfully questioning why it was imprisoned there. The little creature did not seem much roused by the entrance of the visitors, but when her mother said, "Hester, here is the kind lady who sent you the chicken and the picture-books," her eyes brightened, and she pointed to a chair. The mother was beginning to clear the old wooden chair which stood by the pillow, but the child interrupted her with feverish fretfulness. Upon it lay a Sunday School Bible, two or three children's books piled up on some tracts, a cup of toast-water, and a broken mug with flowers, geraniums, jessamines, and a moss-rose,—the sick child's treasury.

"She does so set on those books and flowers, poor patient lamb," said the mother apologetically.

"They are sweet flowers," said Grannie.

"Miss Annie gave them to me," murmured

the child; "she brings some every Sunday." Kate started, and recognized the moss-rose as one from Annie's own tree.

Grannie opened the Bible, and found a little mark on it, in the 51st chapter of Isaiah.

"That was the last chapter Miss Annie read," said the child.

Grannie asked a few simple questions, and found that the blessed news of the free and abundant grace of God had indeed sunk into the heart of the little sufferer herself. She was too much affected to stay long. They were to take tea at the vicarage.

"Grannie," said Kate, after a silence of some duration, as they walked along the street, "I think it was very unkind of Annie not to have told me anything about it. I would not have kept anything from her." And she certainly would not. But Grannie could not join in any reproaches, and she reminded Kate of a verse in the Sermon on the Mount, which made her feel very uncomfortable, for she, poor child, could never have a scheme of kindness in her little head, without imparting it to the whole household. But she promised not to betray this discovery.

They came to the old-fashioned Vicarage House, with its red coat faced with white, passed the sphinxes on the pillars without questioning them, mounted the steps, and entered the hall. Mrs. Fielding was at the Sunday School, Mr. Fielding in his study. They passed through the house into the garden, a large oblong piece of ground, with a stone fountain, green with moss and damp, in the centre of the grass-plot, where gold and silver fish glanced in and out of the shadow of a gigantic dolphin. One side was the wholesome kitchen-garden, and beyond, in the paddock, three cows were forming themselves into a cattle-piece on the sunny grass. But all was silent except a low hum, interrupted by little splashes of a soft treble, from the root-house in the corner. And there sate Annie, a great picture Bible on her knee,—a baby brother standing on one side, and a little sister kneeling in front, looking not at the pictures, but at Annie's face, as she told them in her childish way how good God was, and how the blessed Saviour loved them all. Grannie took Annie's place, and talked to them all until tea-time. Her heart was very full of love to the little creature who seemed entering on so solemn a pilgrimage so early, knowing so little what was to come, but she said nothing more than ordinary. Mr. Fielding was too dreamy, and Mrs. Fielding too busy, to have noticed the little girl as anything more than quiet and amiable, and Grannie would not for the world have withdrawn the flower from the shade which drew out its color and perfume, and yet left it fresh. But she prayed with intense earnestness that evening to Him who carries the lambs of the flock in His bosom.

Kate meanwhile felt half reverent and half aggrieved at Annie. "Dear Grannie," she said, "I am afraid Annie will not live long, she is so like the little good children in the story-books."

"And I think and trust," said Grannie, smiling gravely, "that God will give Annie a long life, as she has so early offered it to Him."

But Kate's own resolution?

She had thought prayer would weave a kind of magic spell about her, wrapping her in invulnerable calm from all the attacks of her old enemies; and she found it necessary to watch and fight as well as pray,—and that her prayers themselves had so often to be for forgiveness,—she grew discouraged. At the end of the week she was so little further on than at the beginning. Nevertheless the force of the purpose was long in spending itself, and might have lasted much longer, had not Kenneth come home and called her "meek" and demure, and laughed her resolutions and penitences away. And so Kate fell gradually back into her old position. But Kenneth never teased Annie. No one ever did. It was so easy for Annie to be good. And Kate began sometimes to pity herself, and to look on goodness as the prerogative of a few, like beauty. Yet she knew better, and at times aimed higher; and even the defeat of good resolutions was silently working for her good. The soil was turned over to the air and light, even if the seeds of that season seemed to perish; the very frost which bound up the earth and hardened it against cultivation, being compelled to work for the gracious purposes of the Omnipotent One.

IV.

TRANSITIONS.

CHILDHOOD, like the robe of summer mist under which the flowers open, was slowly falling off from the children. The drop of water which had hung trembling in the flower-cup with all heaven reflected in it, fell into the stream below, and from a world became a drop, yet a drop in the great river. The island which had been such an empire, became a little island in the river,—the corner of the kitchen-garden sunk from an Utopia into a mere corner of the kitchen-garden,—and even Eastwood and the Vicarage, from a territory like the "World known to the Ancients," bordered by impenetrable wildernesses and nothing, became two houses in and near the disfranchised town of Milbourne. And at the same time, while the beautiful dream of childhood became a shadow, the great world beyond it grew more and more into a vast reality, rising slowly and grandly before their awakening hearts, like a great mountain, with its fresh pastures and solemn forests and snowy top glowing in the sunrise, which in the twilight has seemed to hover over our dreams as a ghost.

Nature grew from a play-ground into a treasury full of the riches of God, and of His rejoicing creatures joining in chorus of welcome around the hearts of the children. Books, from things to say lessons from, or arithmometers on which to count rules of grammar—living companions, interpreters of nature and of their own hearts; music and drawing, from finger exercises on the piano or straight lines, became sources of power and joy.

Yet it was all twilight, the dimness of the unknown adding infinitely to the beauty and delight of what was seen. Themselves scarcely conscious of any change except of an expanding of all things around them—externally little difference to be seen, save that Kate grew more angular and awkward, and Annie very tall and thin and shapeless, her large soft eyes looking up as trustfully and earnestly as ever, and both were somewhat quieter. The world of literature, history, and nature, man's thoughts and deeds, and God's works, opened to them with a delicious feeling that they had found something inexhaustible; but of the actual world, so called, with its petty cares and struggles, and its great perplexities and responsibilities, they knew as little as ever. They had never either of them been thrown into that miniature likeness of the world, a large school, and had not been introduced at any children's balls, so that they were very simple and childlike in many things, and had nothing to come between their little loving home-circle, and the world of great thinkers and workers, poets, conquerors, patriots, and statesmen beyond. They had read Schiller and Manzoni, and Kate was a general champion of all unfortunate princes and oppressed nations, a partisanship which sometimes involved her in very opposite political opinions, as she would be a hot Jacobite in behalf of Charles Edward, and an enthusiastic revolutionary patriot in the cause of Kosciuzsko or Silvio Pellico. And Kenneth did not fail to take advantage of this anomaly in the frequent political discussions held during his months at home, promoted now from Christmas holidays to long vacations. Annie's heroes were of a quieter kind, martyrs and poets, and were chosen with more reference to their moral qualities, and she could not consent to take very strong views in favor of Bonaparte, even at St. Helena; but they both agreed in devotion to Francis Xavier and Gustavus Adolphus. For, in all this joyous spring of life, Annie retained her faith and joy in the yet wider and happier life beyond. Let the earth expand as it might, the heavens were infinite above and around all,—and to Annie the heavens were brought near, by faith in the One Divine and Human Person, slain, and risen, and exalted, who is the worship and joy of all their hosts,—and yet loved and interceded *for her.* Kate was by no means destitute of religious feeling; on the contrary, she felt intensely by impulses, though often, poor child, her intermittent bursts of feeling were rather like hot Geysers than fresh streams, and seemed to leave her heart drier and harder than they found it. But her religion consisting not in faith in a living Redeemer, and the possession of an imperishable treasure, but in efforts to be something she knew she ought to be, and feel something she knew she ought to feel; in other words, instead of looking to Him who bears away burdens, being in itself the heaviest burden of all, she was happier without it; and not having otherwise any sorrow or care, nor having felt the chill of the shadow of death, she was very cheerful and bright, and the life and sunshine of her home.

Jean's school-room reign was over, but there were masters to be prepared for, and drawings to be finished, and doors of which Jean's had provided them with the keys to be opened; magic doors of German and Italian literature, leading to Aladdin's gardens of flowers which were jewels, and singing fountains and talking birds. And Kate would sketch by the river, whilst Annie read; or Kate would read with kindling face of Wilhelm Tell or James Fitzjames, whilst Annie sketched illustrations which Kate thought quite equal to Retzch, and every one thought fanciful and pretty—a talent cultivated of old for the amusement of her little brothers and sisters. Their enthusiasm was usually devoted to deeds of heroism, friendship, and patriotism; the love-scenes, unless redeemed by some extraordinary self-sacrifice, they thought very tiresome and foolish, an opinion in which they met with no discouragement. Annie, however, was more disposed to interest in such matters than Kate, and occasionally, when alone, would not hurry over the tender passages with quite so much impatience, nor without a kind of sweet undefined wonder at what this unknown absorbing feeling might be; but she spoke less of the subject even than Kate. Mrs. Fielding said, and perhaps believed, that such things were all nonsense; only Grannie had one day spoken of love, in Annie's hearing, as the deepest and tenderest feeling that can stir the heart, leading to the holiest and most perfect relationship given to man. Annie mused on the contradiction, and kept her musings to herself; but to both the cousins, in their frequent discussions of the future, it seemed above all a sphere of joyous activity—a mountain of God which they were to climb in exhilarating morning air, every step making the view wider and the air purer. Annie, moreover, wrote occasional poems and hymns, full of opening flowers, and sunset and sunrise, and fragrant breezes, and gushing streams, and spring and autumn, and such images as to older people have become almost as lifeless and as much a matter of course as the Dictionary of Poetical Terms, compiled by the old Northern Bards, but to her were as fresh as the wild flowers and the moorland streams which inspired them; and Grannie very much admired them, and entertained secret hopes that English literature would be illustrated by the authoress. Kate wondered infinitely at this faculty, never having been able, even in an heroic ode she once attempted to Leonidas, to get beyond the second rhyme; but in proportion to her incapacity was her ecstatic admiration of every production of Annie's, which indeed, but for her, would never have been known to any one.

The relations with Jean continued friendly, especially since the close of the school-room era, strictly so called. Kate had an affectionate respect for Jean's orderly and upright character, much deepened since she had ceased to look on it as a model; and Jean, having conceded to Kate a somewhat different standard from her own, had a quiet pleasure in her buoyant spirits, although, on the whole, she was not altogether easy about her progress—and Kate never drew a head of Minerva. She also took an eldersisterly interest in keeping Kate as tidy as circumstances would admit, in pinching her bonnets round, and putting her shawls straight—delicate attentions, which Kate appreciated afterwards, but tolerated at the moment with the spirit of a martyr. Jean had entered by degrees on the general superintendence of the household, one key of office after another falling from her mother's hands into hers, until it was difficult to say what Mrs. Cameron did (Mrs. Fielding, indeed, never could make out), and yet the household economy could not have gone on without her. She fulfilled every negative duty perfectly, she kept at home, loved her husband, and loved her children, and although she seldom exercised much positive control in the way of checking or directing anything, her presence was in itself a good influence, soft and fragrant as a languid spring day—her reverent piety was a silent check to levity—her expansive kindliness was a blight to domestic quarrels or ill-natured criticism—and it was pleasant to know, that in a certain corner by the drawing-room fireside, in a certain easy-chair by a certain cosy little work and reading-table, there was always one to unburden every little project or trouble on, from a stitch dropped in a complicated pattern of knitting to an insurrection in the kitchen, or a case of distress amongst the poor. How much less Mrs. Cameron did than she might have done, or was than she might have been, was another question, a question few of us can answer without trembling.

Annie and Kate were as inseparable as ever. To their plays had succeeded long rambles in lanes and over heath and moorland, botanizing, sketching, or oftener talking on an inexhaustible variety of subjects with an unwearied freshness of interest, subjects which accumulated from the evening separation to the morning, and could only be finished by Annie's sometimes remaining the night, when, after a hundred deceptive closes and reiterated good-nights, the first gray streaks of morning would frighten them to sleep.

Annie taught in the Sunday-school, but Kate could not be induced to take a class: she said she was not good enough, and she was not very fond of her aunt Fielding, and did not relish the idea of being under the immediate supervision of her keen eyes. Mrs. Cameron did not interfere, she was content to watch the development of her children's characters, as she watched the flowers in her conservatory, occasionally sup-

ANNIE AND HER SABBATH SCHOOL CLASS.

Two Vocations. p. 70.

plying a little water, or a prop, if needed; her system of government was strictly *laissez faire.* Mrs. Fielding's on the contrary, was paternal in the Russian sense, not a single point being left to manage itself; and Mrs. Fielding's six children were diligently instructed how to think, how to speak, how to look, how to sit, how to stand, how to eat, how to play, how to be grateful; and the result was, that Mrs. Fielding's six children, from the baby upwards, were the most exemplary and impenetrable children to be met with anywhere—mind, heart, and manners all in strict uniform; and very decided were her denunciations of the contrary system, or no-system. "Jean Cameron was certainly an amiable girl—but time would show."

Mrs. Cameron also was not without misgivings as to what would come out of the chaos of Kate's character. Kenneth had lately brought from Oxford sundry little books with carved bindings, red lines, and angels with wings and glories, and various mysterious symbols therein, which Annie enjoyed on account of their poetry and beauty —and Kate on account of many satirical sayings and descriptions, which she thought applicable to her aunt Fielding. Mrs. Cameron had objected to these importations, and one day consulted Grannie as to the propriety of prohibiting them.

"I have no great confidence in the effect of Expurgatory Indexes," was the reply. "All faith must pass through conflicts. All truth in this fallen world must be Protestant. I think, however, as far as may be, I would discourage *books*, although I would not shrink from the *subject*, but when the books cannot be avoided, speak of the good and evil in them plainly and candidly."

"But," said Mrs. Cameron, "I cannot prevent Kate's seeing such works in other houses, nor keep them by any means from Kenneth."

"It is too true. But, above all, convince

your children of your sympathy. Let them confide their errors, if they are led into them, to you; read the books which mislead them, but read your Bible more. Pray for them, and with them. And yourself, Catharine, have confidence in truth."

"I am not equal to controversy," said Mrs. Cameron languidly; "I suppose I must do as you said, let the thing take its course."

"Indeed, dear Catharine, I said no such thing. I think almost everything rests with you. The lips of a mother with truth on her side give weight to logic which might not pass at the universities. My belief is, you know, that the most penetrating ministry of the gospel is in the hand of Christian mothers." And on the strength of this advice Mrs. Cameron talked for an hour the next Sunday with Kenneth on the subject; but finding his arguments cleverer than hers, she could not help admiring them; and contenting herself with conceding a little, in order to convince him of her candor, and entering a protest against what she could not receive, she relapsed into her usual quiescent state; whilst Kenneth on his part took the course of avoiding the question before his mother, and writing to her from college of his studies and society, to the exclusion of his opinions —a course which Mrs. Cameron rather liked, as it kept her mind easy, and enabled her to read his letters to the family without comment; whilst, as she continued in her own letters to allude occasionally to her brother's sermons, and say some Christian words, she had no idea that she was gradually relinquishing that most precious and sacred of trusts—the inmost heart's confidence of her son. Meanwhile Mrs. Fielding did strictly prohibit all reading or discussion on the question, took Kenneth's suspected presents away from Annie, and locked them up in a cupboard in her own room; and in lieu thereof issued a series of tracts on Popery, and tales of the persecutions practiced in nunneries, which made Kate a zealous defender of the calumniated Church of Rome, and had on Annie no effect whatever, she having never derived anything further from the obnoxious books than an additional love to the services of the church, and a somewhat sentimental attachment to ecclesiastical architecture, which made pretty back-grounds for her etchings. Satire was not in the gentle girl's nature; and as to despising the Independent minister, or the Methodist class-reader, who read the Bible with the poor she visited, and spoke of the love of Christ to the children, no book ever written could have persuaded her to that.

V.

ENDINGS AND BEGINNINGS.

About this time it was formally announced to Kate that Jean was *engaged*, tidings which overpowered her with very mixed emotions. She was sorry to think of losing Jean; she was secretly in a state of tremulous exultation at the idea of the excitement and change, and general promotion of everybody. Jean herself and the whole family seemed to her exalted into another sphere by the intelligence. Jean was to be a wife, a real mistress of her own house, the rectoress of a parish. This reflected glory would have been enough; but the same event would make her the eldest daughter—Miss Cameron. She wondered if mamma would let her make tea, and keep the keys. And these conflicting feelings produced a series of conflicting effects. At first she cried, she could not tell why, inasmuch as Jean was not to remove more than four miles away; then she became marvellously quiet, and felt a kind of awe of Jean, as if she were surrounded by some spell; then, as Mr. More, of whom she had previously known nothing but that he wore a gown and preached sermons, began to bestow on her those little presents and playful attentions which are the portion on such occasions of younger sisters, her spirits became exuberantly high, and occasioned sundry discomfitures to Jean; and finally she subsided into a fusion and alternation of all these states of mind. Meanwhile Jean took things very composedly, and set a very good example, as she always had done, to her sister and cousin, only occasionally indulging in little unusual bursts of tenderness to them, which Kate received with a mixture of gratitude and wonder; for in her own way Jean was very happy, although her feelings did not interfere with her precision in the performance of accustomed duties, or her presence of mind in remembering what quantity of tea and sugar everybody liked, or her judgment in choosing any article of her trousseau, from her walking boots to her wedding bonnet. Then came the wedding-day—to Kate, as to novelists, an era beyond which nothing was to be seen—to Jean, with her calm heart, a kind of Sunday, commencing a new week of earnest working-days—to Mrs. Cameron, a calling back of so much. For bridesmaids there were two sisters of Mr. More's, who being past twenty and very grave, seemed to Kate fifty—and two of Mrs. Fielding's little girls—and occupying a medium position between the two, and younger and fresher than either, were Kate and Annie. It was not quite so merry as Kate had expected. Mrs. Cameron cried, and Grannie cried, which was very solemn, and Annie cried, and Kate felt that she was very unfeeling not to cry;

but between the unusually long toilet and toilet admonitions to be sustained from Nurse in the morning, and the two Miss Mores, and the going to church, Kate was altogether too much awe-stricken for any such outburst of emotion. Then Jean, although very pale, looked so serene and happy, and the whole scene had been so long expected and was so soon over, that in the afternoon Kate could not believe Jean was really married and gone. But in the evening, when she was allowed to take off the white muslin dress and bonnet and resume her everyday frock, and, not knowing what to do, went listlessly into the school-room to fetch a book, and saw Jean's chair and writing-desk, the reality rushed upon her, and she clasped her hands on the desk and buried her head in them, and burst into a flood of such tears as she had never wept before. All her contradiction of Jean's plans, her inattention, her manifold naughtiness, rose magnified before her, and Jean's calm, peaceful ways on the other side;—she felt as if she had ill-treated an angel, and never, never now could she make up for anything. For the first time in her life something had irrevocably passed away, and she wept and thought and looked around, and then hid her face, wept, and sobbed again. At length she resolved to see if she could find her mother, and pour out all the tide of her grief and remorse and resolutions on her, when the door opened gently, and Grannie came in.

"Annie has been looking for you everywhere," she said; and then, as the sobs came afresh, she sat down, whilst Kate knelt at her feet, and hid her flushed, tearful face on her shoulder.

"Oh Grannie, I have been so ungrateful to dear Jean—I have not loved her half enough."

The tears of the old lady fell on the head of the child. She had known so many irrevocable losses—so many seasons when the thought of what might have been done, and never could be, had weighed upon her heart. But she spoke of what *might be* done, of Jean's return, and all Kate must be to Mrs. Cameron, until the tears were dried, and Kate's heart began again to bound with a thousand bright plans and hopes; and when she had become calm, and Annie had stolen gently in and taken Grannie's other hand, she spoke to them both for some time in her earnest loving way. Then rising and seeing the sunset from the window, she proposed to rejoin the rest of the party.

Kate turned to go, but Annie lingered and whispered,

"I think marriage is very like death, Grannie."

"How can you say anything so dismal and unkind, Annie!" exclaimed Kate.

"I did not mean it to be dismal," said Annie coloring. "I only meant the leaving the old home and going to a new home we do not know, and yet love"——

Grannie kissed the little girl's forehead, and said, looking almost reverently into her earnest up-turned eyes,—"And to be with Him whom, having not seen, we love, who has purchased and is preparing that blessed home for us."

"I think that was what I meant, Grannie —I do not think it is dismal."

But Kate did not like the thought at all, and her tears began to flow again. Annie kissed them away; and clasping their arms round each other, they followed Grannie, full of that tender love of theirs, which united the home-familiarity of a sister's with the choice and sympathy of friendship.

Kate's heart was so softened and expanded that evening, that it even overflowed to her aunt Fielding and the Miss Mores.

VI.

THE SCHEME.

For the first time Kate felt what it was to be entirely free;—no one to tell her when to practice, or draw, or walk; no one to interrupt an absorbing study or an interesting story, by tiresome suggestions that it was time to do this or that. Everything was too fresh and her heart too joyous to feel such freedom from duties to be the heavy slavery it is. Mrs. Cameron had her housekeeping arrangements in the morning; after these she needed rest, and some desultory book of travels or history made easy; in the afternoon, she was often at Weston Vicarage with Jean; and in the evening, they either had music or Kate read aloud.

Nothing was further from Kate's intention

than to be idle. The first Monday after Jean's marriage, when her little personal property had all been collected and dispatched to Weston, and there arranged and disposed with affectionate anticipations of the pleasure Jean would have in recognizing her old friends in their new spheres, and the first letters had been received from the travellers, quieting those at home by the reality of post-marks and written names into a sense of the reality of the change, Kate devoted the whole morning to making a scheme for the employment of her time, after the most approved recommendations. It was mapped with rubrical precision, with red lines to divide the hours, and black lines for the half-hours; not a moment was to be lost, all the old studies were to be energetically kept up, and new ones added. Having finished this, and walked to Milbourne, and there purchased a second-hand Hebrew Grammar and Bible, and an Elementary Treatise on Chemistry, and a Diary, in which the doings of the day were duly recorded, she retired to rest, full of satisfaction at the work she had done and was to do. The next two days were wet, and every hour was strictly filled with its allotted occupations. On the third, Mrs. Cameron came into the school-room just as Kate had established herself at her desk, flanked by an imposing array of dictionaries and elementary treatises, with three open letters in her hand.

"Invitations?" exclaimed Kate, in a deprecatory tone.

"Yes, my dear, and I feel too unhinged to answer them."

"Very well, dear mother; if you will leave them on the table, I will answer them before post-time."

"That will not do; the messengers are waiting."

Kate looked round imploringly on all her intellectual apparatus, and Mrs. Cameron answered the look.

"Never mind, Kate; I see you are busy.

I will not interrupt you. It is so difficult to get into the way of doing all these little things Jean used to do."

Kate's books were laid aside in a moment. The sealing-wax and paper were fetched, the letters written and dispatched, and Kate sat herself again to her pursuits; but she felt unsettled, and after toiling through an hour or two, she remembered some imperative want in Milbourne, and the day was broken. The diary was scantily filled that evening, but Kate consoled herself with thinking it was her misfortune, and not her fault.

On the fourth day Annie was at Eastwood, —and with an expedition to the hills, reading and chatting, the hours passed like magic.

With all the more zeal Kate took out her scheme on Friday, but the first hour was scarcely over when the servant came in with a new book from the Reading Society. It was not particularly interesting nor instructive, but it was new, and in a day or two it must be forwarded, and so the hours glided away on the slow current of its pages; and when Mrs. Cameron came in to tell her the carriage was waiting for a drive, Kate felt aggrieved at the interruption. She was on the point of beginning something, but it was too late; and as they drove, she communicated her difficulties to her mother.

"My poor child, why should you worry yourself about your scheme? You know it is only your own manufacture, and you have all your time to yourself."

Kate acquiesced, but she felt a secret consciousness of the necessity of law to make freedom free, and she said, "I wish I was like Annie. She has so much to do, she has scarcely time for anything! I think the happiest thing in the world must be to have just a little too much to do."

Mrs. Cameron could not at all comprehend the luxury, and the subject dropped.

On Saturday the scheme was again resumed, but in the midst of some difficulty of construction in the Hebrew, the subtle question arose for the first time, "What is the good of all this? Who will be the better for your knowing this?" And although she answered it by many sound arguments, a languor crept over her efforts; and rising before the prescribed time, she went out to consult Grannie with a kind of superstitious faith in her magic power of answering all the riddles of life. The day was warm, with a bracing wind; and between the exhilaration of a brisk walk, and the stirring of her heart by the movements of all the blithe and busy creatures out of doors, the leaves, flowers, and even clouds sailing like white-winged vessels before the wind, freighted with pearls for some impoverished land, her difficulties all seemed to vanish. The whispers of conscience and of ennui became faint as the breath of a breeze in the distance, amidst the "songs" with and "without words" of nature, and her own fresh and hopeful heart, so that when she came to

Grannie she scarcely knew her errand. "I have been very unhappy all the morning, Grannie," she said, her bright face contradicting her words.

"What is the matter?"

"Nothing, I believe," was the laughing reply, "but my scheme. I have made a scheme for every half-hour of every day. It has been weighing on me like a night-mare. I think I was not made for schemes, Grannie. I must just take things as they come."

"You were made for duties, dear Kate," said Grannie seriously; "and to fulfill any of these we need self-denial and steadfastness of purpose."

"Well, dear Grannie, so I thought; and as no one has chalked out a course of life for me, I marked out one for myself, and I think if I continue it a few days longer it will quite spoil my disposition. It has been the cause of my very nearly making mamma cry three times, and of making me very cross continually."

"Dear child, God has a scheme for each of our lives, but as we cannot see that, it is well for us prayerfully to make some plan for ourselves; only remembering, that when interruptions come in the form of duties, we must not fret, but look on them as a part of God's invisible scheme for us, crossing ours for a space, and blotting it out—not meant to make us lay aside the whole."

Kate looked thoughtful and half-satisfied; she shrank from mentioning her great difficulty of the object and end of all her labors. Besides that, it had already shrunk into a very thin voice. She returned to Eastwood; and the scheme, instead of meeting a violent end at her hands, died a natural death on the arrival of her brother the next week.

VII.

NEW DIVINING RODS AND OLD FOUNTAINS.

BOTH Kate and Mrs. Cameron observed a change in Kenneth. He talked less about the Catholic Ideal, and seemed less possessed by the worship of dead centuries—apparently retaining little of his former opinions, but a quiet contempt for all beside, only betrayed, however, in occasional expressions. Kate had never felt her brother such a companion; he seemed interested in all she thought and did, and even volunteered to give Annie and herself lessons in Greek, after he had laughed her out of Hebrew.

The evening after he arrived there was a Missionary meeting. Kate, as usual, had her warm heart quite enkindled by the thoughts and facts brought before her.

"How nice it was to see the little children bringing their pence, was it not, Kenneth?"

"No," said Kenneth; "I do not think it was at all nice. It seems to me like robbery for burnt-offering. At least let us give in our proportion. It is now, however, I believe, much as it was in the days of Christ. Only those whose all is a mite give it."

"But our Lord did not reject that mite," said Annie, gently. "He did not say, Put it back again; you will want it for your own food to-morrow."

"Yes, indeed, Annie, if it is really voluntary; but who will say that these poor children's mites are? If aunt Fielding were away, how many of those half-pence would find their way to the apple-stall, and how many to the missionary-box?"

"I know three of my class give because they love to help," she said.

"Or because they love you, Annie," was the sceptical rejoinder.

"How earnestly the deputation spoke!" observed Annie, gently putting aside, according to her wont, a course of argument she did not like.

"He has abundance of practice," said Kenneth, drily. "It is astonishing," he added, "to see what sensible people will receive as eloquence at religious meetings. But, perhaps, it is well there should be such a charitable asylum for destitute phrases and worn-out ideas."

"When the heart is really warm and fresh," said Annie, gently, "does not whatever it touches become so?"

"I am afraid my heart has never received such a miraculous gift of raising the dead," said Kenneth. "However, everything has its use, they say. The societies are admirable exhausting engines, and do instead of balls for those who disapprove of such vanities. For myself, as a matter of business, I cannot see the use of laboring for two hours to prove what a few minutes' plain statement ought to effect as well. If it is true that 'the eighty millions of India' are perishing for lack of teaching we can bestow, those who believe it ought surely not to heed declamations, and stories, and picturesque illustrations to excite their sympathies."

"But," interposed Annie, "we are not what we ought to be, we are so weak, and so forgetful of what we owe."

Kenneth did not reply; they had reached the Rectory door. Kate felt an undefined chill and doubt thrown over her by this conversation, too undefined to be combated, yet subtle enough to penetrate far and deep.

Annie remembered Kenneth's words in that evening hour, when she recalled all the day's words and works. It was her custom not to revolve such things in the darkness of her own heart, but to bring them at once to the light. And she said, in meekness and lowliness of heart, "We are indeed triflers in thy service, O our Father; we do not let the realities around us and above us sink enough into our hearts. We are between life and death; daily some are ascending from our midst into heaven, and some are descending into hell, and yet we dream and loiter. Yet we do believe; help thou our unbelief." And her faith burned the brighter for the doubt it consumed.

Happily and quietly the days passed. Kate did not make so much progress as Annie in Greek; she could not enter into the stately beauty which Annie and Kenneth seemed to discover in those old Greek classics, and she found the grammar and construction very tiresome; so after nine or ten lessons she left them to pursue their way alone, and took up some of Kenneth's prohibited theological and philosophical books, German and English, carried on by the same sense of adventure and danger which had tempted her through the unknown wilds of their valley in days of yore. Annie, on the other hand, declined all invitations into this unexplored territory. She did not feel strong enough to cope with the race of giants who were said to have their fastnesses there; and said to Kate, "I can never learn enough of truth, I have not time to learn error."

Kenneth respected her timidity, which he thought feminine, although weak. The results on the cousins were as different as the progress. Kate certainly did not consciously relinquish one point of her creed, but she held all less firmly. She thought Kenneth went too far in many things, although she rather enjoyed hearing him say anything startling, especially before aunt Fielding. She did not herself laugh at the idea of conversion, but her sense of the need of such a change in herself became less and less vivid. She did not question the inspiration of any part of the Bible, but she read all of it less frequently, and with less conviction of its being the message from the Almighty God to her own soul. At the same time she dwelt much on the necessity of reality, and gave up many forms of religious expression, which Kenneth stigmatized as the phraseology of a party, or "Hebrew idioms;" and was especially busy and indignant at the inconsistencies of Christians.

Annie, meanwhile receiving the Word of God day by day as the lamp to her feet, as well as the revelation of heaven, and walking in its light in meekness and fear, grew daily in peace and love, so that Kenneth often seemed to enjoy her earnest disapproval more than Kate's sympathy. He thought her, perhaps, very short-sighted and feminine in her judgments. And Annie never claimed for herself anything more.

There was a school-tea at the Rectory garden, an opportunity which Mrs. Fielding always used for gathering together all the incongruous and inharmonious people in the parish, who could not be drawn together in any other way, and of paying off a number of social debts. She was herself peculiarly great and gracious on the occasion. A mixture of contrivance and worldliness there might be about these gatherings; nevertheless they were pleasant annual festivals, which Annie and Kate had loved, and still loved, from the mere habit of looking forward to them from their earliest childhood, in company with the three hundred children, who were (at least to them) the object of the evening. There were so many happy associations connected with them, from the days when Kate and Annie, then "the children" of the two families, used to join in some of the plays, and totter with the burden of the great cake-basket, and carry fragments to the sick children the next day, and think it a great honor and promotion to be allowed to carry round the jugs of tea (a dignity Kate was not considered eligible to until two years after Annie)—to this evening, when so many of the little creatures reverenced Miss Fielding as their patient and loving teacher. Kate, however, felt more shy with the children that evening; she had few personal acquaintances among them, and her heart, not buoyed up by the joy of living earnestly for others, felt heavy and censorious. She watched the little distinctions and dignities and jealousies which the classes of English society in the most minute grades of difference are too apt to set up between them, instead of the definite legal barriers of other times and lands, and overheard her aunt Fielding, after graciously welcoming every one, wonder at the absurd pretensions and finery of the trades-people, until she worked herself up into a cynical conviction that the world and the Church were equally hollow and empty, and that there was no sincerity or consistency upon earth. Kenneth was not near to vent her discoveries on; Annie was as happy and as busy as possible, gliding in and out everywhere like a sunbeam, as quiet, and leaving just a track behind; and Kenneth persisted in thinking the cake-baskets too heavy for her, and the tea-distribution too laborious.

No one noticed her, and she sat like an Undine on the edge of the fountain. Kenneth came and stood beside her for a moment. "Why must people go abroad, or to the middle ages, for the poetry of life?" he said, in a low voice.

"Because, I suppose," she replied, "they are far off and past to us. I have no doubt the people who lived in them did the same."

Kenneth was prevented from discussing the point by the occurrence of a catastrophe at that moment. The long form on which the smaller children sate had been converted into a see-saw by the sudden rising of all its occupants to sing a concluding grace, with the exception of a hapless little wight at the end, who, with his small hands full of his mug and a superfluous piece of cake, had been precipitated screaming to the ground. The compassionate crowd who rushed to his rescue soon, however, discovering that the chief anxiety was connected with "grandmother" and the "new frock," his tears were soon dried with the aid of certain unmedical contents of Grannie's pocket—and the little ones were silenced again. From the little voices, somewhat thickened in quality by the previous entertainment, arose on the still evening air the concluding grace; and Mr. Fielding's kind but supine feelings quite overflowed on the occasion, and he made a little speech about the advantages of the rising generation, and the benevolence of the full-grown generation, and the progressive regeneration of everything, which sent every one home in the best humor with themselves and the school. Kate watched it all from her watery throne—the little group in the sunshine at the edge of the lengthening shadow, which was etching the roofs and chimney tops in irregular lines on turf and shrub—uncle Fielding with his gray hair leaning down to speak to Grannie, both of them very much affected, and Annie on the other side looking up with her bright face to Kenneth, and pointing out to him some favorite among the children—the quiet field, and cattle in sunshine beyond—it was most picturesque, in spite of the people being dressed out of the *Modes de Paris* as far as the Milbourne dressmakers could translate it, instead of out of an illuminated romance or missal—and quite poetical—to the heart.

At least Grannie thought so as well as Kenneth; he, perhaps, through the magic of a new tenderness, and she in the perpetual magic of a heart kept by Divine peace, and inhabited by heavenly love.

And Annie's old Nurse came and said, wiping her eyes, "Oh, Miss Kate, is it not like a foretaste of paradise, as dear master said—such beautiful rich cake and bread and butter too. And to think I remember you and Miss Annie no bigger than the smallest there, that clap their hands and sing so pretty, in your little white pinnies and blue sashes, dear lambs."

Kate could not help laughing at the lambs

in blue sashes, and the collocation of plum-cake and paradise, and the very sound of her laughter nearly burst the cobwebs of cynicism she had been weaving around her heart; but as she joined Grannie and they turned into the shadow of the house from the depopulated lawn, and she heard Mrs. Fielding through the open window paying and receiving compliments, the shadow fell on her heart again, and she said,

"I have been thinking of the homes of these children, Grannie, and of ours. How little we can do! what a mere strip of rainbow painted on the dark future of their lives such a day as this is!"

"Light and darkness come from within, not from without, dear Kate, and many of those children may have a rainbow spanning their hearts perpetually—a rainbow of essential light and eternal promise—brighter, Kate, perhaps than all your bright home can weave for yours." And her kind eyes, from which years and tears had indeed blotted out the color but not the light, rested tenderly on Kate. But Kate was not disposed for any home thrusts, and she replied,

"I do not believe there is a consistently religious person in the world, Grannie, except you."

"My dear child," Grannie replied, almost startled out of any reply by such an exclusive compliment, "what are you saying? Think of your dear mamma, and Annie, and—"

"They are excellent in their way, I know," interrupted Kate, "but it is their own way. Mamma could not help being kind; aunt Fielding could not help being busy; Annie could not help being everything one would wish her to be, nor Jean being everything she ought to be. But I do not see that religion changes people, gives them what is not in their nature, or takes away from them what is there. I do not see the practical difference between the

Church and the world. I do not see regeneration either in society or individuals."

Grannie was silent a moment; then she said, earnestly, "My child, you need to know histories before you can judge of results. There is a moment when the sun rises, though none may see it; but after that who can say when the first petal opens, or when the icicle becomes a dew-drop, and the dew-drop enters into the life of the flower? There is a moment when the leaf-bud bursts its varnished casing and forces off the old leaf, and spreads its fan to the breeze, but who saw it? You see the dead leaf lying on the earth beneath, and the green leaf fluttering in the air above, and if you had never watched a spring before you might say it was always thus."

"And if I saw the dead leaf lying dead, and the living one green month after month and year after year," she answered, "who could contradict me?"

"Every one who was old enough to remark the babyhood of your very slow and saturnine plant," said Grannie smiling. "Years are not of the same length in all the planets—they are ages in those farthest from the sun. And what would be a life-time to a primrose would seem but a day to an aloė. Have you watched the seasons in your own heart, Kate?"

"There are no seasons, Grannie," said Kate, "where there is no sun; and if that has not risen, what is there to watch?"

Grannie would have pursued the subject; but Kate at that moment hearing voices near, and not wishing just then to be persuaded out of her difficulty, welcomed the interruption.

And Grannie, meditating on this conversation, whilst it led her to humble herself for those inconsistencies which she appropriated as her own, nevertheless rejoiced to see any fermentation in Kate's mind, even though the immediate product might be mere disturbance.

VIII.

CONCESSIONS AND THEIR CONSEQUENCES.

ANNIE was sitting quietly reading one morning, after having heard her little brothers their Latin lessons and dispatched them to school, when Kate and Kenneth came in. One of the windows was open, and on a flower-stand in the other stood a camellia and some early violets, especial pets of Annie. The room was of that maid-of-all-work character so requisite in all large families, doing duty for any of the regular apartments when they were disabled or overworked, and fulfilling besides a variety of miscellaneous offices of its own. In addition to all this it was Annie's—sanctum it could not be called, to which no feet were profane—but her own especial domain, and as such Kenneth declared it had a character distinct from all the rest of the house. On the old piano was usually a fresh nosegay, witnessing and breathing of rambles in woods and fields; in the window, some choice flowers the old gardener took delight in nursing for "Miss Annie;" on the table, books and drawings. And to-day the sweet air and sunshine came in over the garden and made it peculiarly pleasant.

Kenneth took up the book Annie had laid down. It was one of Baxter's. Annie felt herself blush, and blushed deeper with the shame of blushing at any occupation which she knew was a good one. She would not have cared if it had been the Bible, but she shrunk from her cousin's quiet smile as he laid it silently down again, and began to turn over some of her drawings.

"It is of no use your trying to make yourself a Puritan, Annie," he said, holding up triumphantly an etching of St. Elizabeth of Bohemia, embodying a legend he had told her the day before. "You will never be able to clothe the world in sackcloth and ashes, however honest your intentions may be."

Annie resolved to be heroic, and entered on a warm defence of the Puritans, and the beauty of earnestness.

"Very good indeed, I will allow you to be a Puritan in Charles II.'s times, if you can restore them; meantime you must be yourself, and come with Kate on an expedition over the hills to the Giant's Bath."

It was a wild moorland excursion through tangled brakes and over the crisp, short moorland grass, and up broken rocky hills, and by the side of moorland streams, where the clear water was colored a rich brown by the earth below, and broken into short hurrying cascades over the granite stones, which served the cousins for bridges. Kate had always been a more daring climber than Annie, which made it necessary for Kenneth to linger behind with his cousin. Besides,

Kate had taken to geologising, and was very busy with hammer and basket—a pleasure Annie could never enter into. She disliked breaking nature to pieces to see what was inside, although the great revelations of every science were full of interest to her. She loved to watch the great rocks as features of nature when sunshine swept across them like music and woke them into expression; she knew the dwelling-places and habits of all the common birds and flowers, and welcomed them whenever she met them as old friends, but she had no appreciation for that commercial estimate of her favorites which valued them according to their rarity.

Annie's thoughts, moreover, were busy during that walk with the morning's conversation. She felt ashamed of her own weakness in being half-ashamed of Baxter, and she said, "Did you ever read any of those old divines, Kenneth, that you seem to despise so much?"

"I do not despise any one," replied Kenneth; "they were excellent men in their generation, no doubt."

"But religion is not a thing of fashion and date," she said.

"And yet *you* or uncle Fielding would not exactly deem it the highest exercise of thanksgiving to have praises in your mouth and a two-edged sword in your hands, nor, I think, would you allow yourself to be drowned like that young Scotch girl for refusing to say, 'God save the king!' *Language* changes, Annie, and what is the natural colloquial of one generation becomes either a dead language, or a vulgar dialect to their descendants."

"The flowers change and die, Kenneth, but the light is always fresh."

Kenneth began to suspect she was trying to "do him good," and he replied perversely,

"I cannot follow you into those transcendental regions, Annie. I only know light as it falls in a million colors on things around me, and comes refracted through a frequently foggy atmosphere to my eyes."

"Oh, Kenneth," Annie resumed, after a pause, "I wish you believed as we do; there is such peace in it."

"As *who* do?" he answered carelessly. "Besides," he added, "how can you tell what I believe, Annie? I say the Creed every Sunday with you, and you refuse to read any of the books which you imagine embody my opinions."

"Indeed, I know I should not like them," she said, "and what right have I to put doubts into my heart? I have not strength to be a controversialist."

"Why then bind yourself to a party, and refuse to admit truth except when clothed in one peculiar terminology. But you cannot become a mere partisan, Annie, however honest your intentions—I am quite easy about you; it is not in your nature."

Annie did not reply, and at that juncture Kate returned, exclaiming that she had found a perfect dining-room, and triumphantly displaying her basket full of scientific bits of stone.

Annie meditated seriously over her cousin's words, and began to think she might have been a little too dogmatic and bigoted. In consequence of this conclusion she no longer objected to hearing Kenneth read passages out of sundry religious works, translated and original, which were contraband articles at home.

Beautiful thoughts he introduced to her, some that looked very like the old truths with a slight change of dress; some that, although not altogether true, threw new light on old truths; errors that seemed too good-natured and clever to be roughly handled; beautiful expanded thoughts about God's fatherly goodness to the universe; acute satires on certain antiquated theologians, whose religion was marked out with the precision of a Chinese landscape (whilst in nature there were no outlines), and who consigned souls to the flames as ruthlessly as so many shreds of false doctrines; criticism on peculiarities of expression and inconsistencies of action, which only gave clear utterance to dislikes which had often struggled to the surface of her own mind, and been resolutely chained or conjured down again. So Annie listened, warmly admiring where she could, gently protesting where she could not admire, until Kenneth began to think her mind expanding considerably.

Occasionally these readings would recur at her hours of quiet, and clog the wings of some ascending prayer, or veil with a gauzy cloud some glimpse into the heavens, or enfeeble her words in some earnest exhortation to her Sunday class, or bring up some ghost from the depths of her own imagination between her and the warm sun; but if she did not feel so peaceful when alone, she took more and more pleasure in the society of Kate and Kenneth, and felt less constraint with them. Her motive, she persuaded herself all the while, was to obtain more influence over Kate and Kenneth, and to win their sympathy for her opinions by showing that she could enter into theirs. How far she used the influence thus gained was another question—she always intended to use it. How far the sympathy thus gained would be like what she sought to purchase it with, a courteous toleration rather than an earnest concession—sympathy with her rather than with her faith—she shrank from asking herself.

"Kenneth, I do wish you would give me no more of these misty books," said Mrs. Cameron one morning in an injured tone, closing some objectionable volume; "they leave one in a complete chaos, until one cannot make out what the author believes or what he disbelieves, or what one believes one's-self. I had really rather listen to as many pages of Johnson's Dictionary. It would be much more comprehensible, and just as connected."

"I am sure," exclaimed Mrs. Fielding, coming in through the greenhouse, in a fever of polemical excitement, "things are getting comprehensible and definite enough in some quarters. The new rector of Byland has excavated the rood-loft, and turned round the reading-desk, and is getting the pillars picked and the windows painted, and is teaching the charity children to chant the Psalms. Rank Popery! and I cannot rouse your brother to get up a petition to the archbishop."

"Why will not people let things alone?" said Mrs. Cameron, half peevishly.

"Aunt Fielding would whitewash the flowers and the sky, I believe, if she could," murmured Kate in the window to Kenneth.

"I wonder," he replied, as they stepped into the garden, "if Milton had consulted aunt Fielding about the description of the garden of Eden, what advice she would have given him. I think her ideal of it would have been a walled kitchen-garden."

Annie half smiled as she bent over her crotchet work, but Grannie said gravely,

"I do agree with you, Mrs. Fielding, that nothing is a trifle which leads people to walk by sight rather than by faith; to imagine they are serving God and building up his Church, when they are only ministering to their own taste, and building houses to pray and hear some truths in."

"They should at least," observed Mrs. Cameron, "be tender to the failings of the weaker brethren, as I often tell Kenneth."

"If, indeed," rejoined Grannie, "the weaker brethren are those who prefer reading the truth in God's own words to spelling it in picture-books."

"Grannie is certainly a little severe," thought Annie. At the moment she said nothing, but when afterwards she expressed this feeling, Grannie said, "Perhaps I was harsh, my love. The only safe way to look on these controversies is from above, in lowly communion with God; there with Him in the heavenly sanctuary, and nowhere on earth, is the substance of all these shadows over which we contend—and starve."

IX.

TWO POINTS OF VIEW.

THINGS had been going on prosperously with the cousins. Annie felt sure that Kenneth, if he did not quite agree with her, yet saw the perfect reasonableness of her believing as she did. She wrote hymns and poems free from the expressions which her cousin's fastidious taste objected to, and, by dint of considerable circumlocution, imagined she succeeded in expressing her faith on many points in a way which avoided scandal. In reading with the poor, indeed, she found the old scriptural expressions the only comprehensible ones; and at times the contrast of the two dialects flashed on her consciousness with a painful feeling of insincerity, and a painful fear that in her anxiety to avoid "cant" she was falling into that which constitutes the essence of cant—paying greater attention to words than to things.

One morning, however, at Eastwood, she was startled by Kate's announcing that she was going to a ball the next week.

"A ball, Kate," exclaimed Annie, "will aunt Cameron like it?"

"Mamma does not object to my making the experiment," Kate replied; "how can one prove things without trying them?"

"But it is so thoroughly a worldly amusement."

"How do you know, Annie? What right have you to condemn people in that indiscriminate way? What harm can there be in exercising the faculty of dancing, any more than the faculty of drawing; or in talking in the pauses of a waltz any more than in the pauses of a song? Why should not I dance with as simple a heart in the ball-room as children play in a garden?".

"We are not children, Kate."

"No; but we need recreation."

"Yes; but balls are not a refreshment; they are a toil; and we must draw the line somewhere."

"How can you use such traditional commonplaces? That is just what aunt Fielding said one day, when she was asserting the religious distinction between the acts of wearing flowers inside and outside one's bonnet—the line in that case being the edge of the bonnet."

Annie was driven back on her own earnest feelings.

"But I never could go, Kate. I should not be happy there. What do we want of such laborious amusements? How can we thank God for them, or think peacefully of His presence?"

"That must depend on ourselves," replied Kate; "I *do* wish to go, and expect to amuse myself and other people—a philanthropic object at least."

Annie felt that the root of the question

lay deeper, and that it was in vain to enter further on it then.

She went home, and felt unhappy and unsettled. Had she been narrow-minded in her judgments, and received a code of traditional morality, which had no sanction but circumstances and education? What indeed was the essential difference between a ball and a school-tea at home? Worldliness was mixed up with both—worldly hearts engaged in both. In this perplexity she had recourse once more, with earnest prayer, to her Bible. During the past few days she had read it languidly, and rather as a matter of routine; but now a perplexity met her—the distinction between the Church and the world, the limits between the unlawful and the inexpedient. She longed to find in the Bible some definite rule for every circumstance—some enlarged New Testament code of "Thou shalt nots;" and she found nothing but general principles and cases it seemed uncharitable to apply. It surely was rather severe to compare the meeting of a hundred highly respectable members of the Church of England to dance, with considerable sedateness, to the sound of an orderly military band, to the mob-feast before the temple of an idol, or to bring it under the head of "revelling," or "rioting."

On the morning after the ball she went to Eastwood, not without a secret hope of finding Kate worn out and dissatisfied, and exemplifying vividly the folly of such amusement. But, on the contrary, she found Kate in brilliant health and spirits, full of admiration at the delicious accuracy of the music and the beauty of the whole scene, and full of amusement at whatever could not be admired, and declaring that she had discovered a new faculty in herself, and a new significance in music, and that all nature was an assembly of graceful and happy dancers to the music of their own voices. The higher Kate's spirits rose the lower Annie's sank. She did not like to enter too warmly into it for fear of seeming inconsistent, nor to be indifferent for fear of seeming censorious; and the result was that she was uneasy and constrained. She felt like a culprit before her cousin, and at length left, persuaded that she had, during the whole interview, seemed a perfect exemplication of envy, hatred, malice, and all uncharitableness. She had not proceeded far on her return to the Rectory, when she met Hester Burn, the sick child, now grown into a sickly woman, with a form which still retained its childish proportions, and a face worn by pain and infirmity into premature old age. She had crept out in the sunshine for half an hour. Her little brother, a boyish, rosy contrast to the crippled girl, was with her. She leant on him as a staff. She did not recognize Annie until she came close to her; the unusual light dazzled her weak eyes. But when she looked up and saw who was coming to her, her whole face shone, and her limbs trembled with pleasure. Annie made her sit down on a primrose bank by the side of the green lane, and the boy crept away, well-pleased to be able, without unkindness, to exchange his sober task for the exciting search after birds'-nests, of which the songs on all sides had been painfully reminding him.

Annie sat down beside her; she did not feel as if she had anything bright or comforting to say, but Hester did not need it. She was full of the delight of this unusual glimpse into God's works, and of meeting Miss Annie then and there, and full of thankfulness to Him who she believed guided her steps.

"It seems, Miss Annie, as if the little birds and the flowers and all were singing the Sermon on the Mount to me; those blessed words—consider the fowls of the air and the lilies. How good it was of our Lord to make even the poor dumb creatures talk to us so of Him!"

"Annie's heart and eyes were full—she could not answer, but the spell on her heart was broken—her soul was brought again into communion with her God. The living water she had poured into Hester's heart came back freshly thence to her own, when it was parched and dry. She drank in her need from the vessel she had filled. How often it is in this way that those who water are watered also themselves! Thus, as an old poet said, all creatures drink in turn from one another.

Annie had been on her way to lay her perplexities before Grannie;—now they no longer lay so heavily on her heart, her eye was once more turned upwards instead of inward, and she felt ashamed at having been so long occupied with herself. Nevertheless she pursued her way, and, as she walked, some of the banished perplexities came buzzing in her ears again. She met Grannie at the door. Grannie was full of the sick people she had been visiting, and some interesting letters she had been receiving from foreign missionary stations. Annie was also interested; she thought, however, that Grannie was rather long, and was rejoiced when, after a series of somewhat absent answers, Grannie folded her dispatches, deposited them in her capacious pockets, and said, "Now, my child, tell me about yourself."

Grannie, in common with all very unselfish people, had some tendency to render those around her very much the contrary—but Annie evaded the question.

"I have been to Eastwood."

"And how did Kate enjoy her ball?"

"Extremely," replied Annie, "she says she never enjoyed anything so much in her life."

"Well, I hope she will live to enjoy many things better. Dear child, she would be sure to be liked and admired there, with her bright sunbeam of a face, and a heart to correspond."

Annie thought Grannie treated the whole matter rather lightly, and she said,

"I wish I had such bright spirits as Kate. I am so afraid I give her a gloomy impression of religion. I am really happy, Grannie, but when I saw her just now so gay, it made me quite sad. These things must be right or wrong. Yet I cannot find for Kate or myself any reason or law about them."

"Our laws, dear Annie, must all be written in the heart. They are organic, not merely material laws; mind cannot be fettered from without, like matter, with dead rules; it must be guided from within by living principles."

"But we have a standard by which to judge," Annie suggested. "A living being may be diseased, Grannie, and we need some one to enable us to distinguish between the symptoms of health and disease."

"Undoubtedly, and we have a standard—the Word of God is quick and powerful, and pierceth even to the dividing asunder of joints and marrow—no analytical instrument so fine."

"But in a case like this, for instance, what advice does it give?"

"You have no doubt about your own course, have you, dear Annie?"

"None at all."

"Then do not perplex yourself about other people's duties. I believe God invariably answers through the Bible (our only oracle now), the sincere question, 'What wilt thou have *me* to do?' But you remember the answer given to the question, 'Lord, what shall this man do?'"

Annie was silent for a moment.

"But Kate seems so happy, and talks often with so much love and joy and religious reverence of God and nature, and yet, Grannie, her feelings are so different from mine, and many of those books I love best, I can see she thinks full of empty phraseology and cant, although she often speaks so beautifully and religiously. And she declares dancing may be as much an act of thankfulness in its way as a hymn—a ballroom a place of as simple enjoyment as a garden."

"Dear Annie, again let me beg you to leave Kate's conscience to herself, and the guidance of her life to God. You are satisfied for yourself that such amusements are among the things of the world which minister to our evil nature, and which we are commanded not to love."

"Yet," replied Annie hesitatingly, "I cannot bear that Kate and Kenneth should think me and my faith gloomy and narrow-minded. I am afraid of weakening any influence I might have with them for good."

"My child," said Grannie very earnestly, laying her hand on Annie's arm, "never listen to your heart when it suggests that, for surely that is one of the devil's subtlest lies: 'All this will I give thee, if——.' Believe me, he can give you nothing to use for God. Influence is, I believe, one of the most dangerous and popular idols of the day. Use what you have, my child, use what you have; follow your Saviour with a single heart, and leave Him to give you as much influence as He pleases."

"But I am so unhappy and anxious about Kate."

"Tell your heavenly Father that, my child, and let your anxieties be turned into prayers."

"Yes, but Kate's arguments have so much truth in them. And it is so difficult to define logically the boundaries between one employment and amusement and another."

"Not only difficult, I should think, but impossible. There is no answering the question, Annie, How far may I venture into the world? but by this other question, How near can I live to God?"

X.

THE VICARAGE.

Two conversations were going on simultaneously at Eastwood and Milbourne Rectory. What a strange whirlpool of contradictory words there must be at the focus at which the contemporary sayings of any circle meet! Annie was drawing, Mr. Fielding reading Hooker, Mrs. Fielding's active mind much too little engrossed by her sewing to suffer others to pursue their occupations at peace.

"Kate returned yesterday from London; how was she looking, Annie?"

"Very well," replied Annie, "and very bright and blooming."

"All excitement, entirely excitement," rejoined Mrs. Fielding. "She will suffer for it by and by."

Annie did not answer.

"Did she speak much of all the gaiety she has been in?"

"She spoke most of some Italian singers."

"That she heard at the opera, I suppose?"

"I believe so."

"Do you hear, Edward?"

"I did, my dear."

"You remember how I urged you to use your influence against that fancy?"

"I do, my dear."

"I wonder how your sister can justify herself. Well, I am thankful I said and did what I could."

Mr. Fielding replied in a tone of quiet satire, which was the only offensive weapon he ever used, and that only when driven to extremities,—"Very true, my love. You can justify yourself completely in this matter, and may thank God like one of old." And rising abruptly, he proposed a walk to Weston Vicarage with Annie, to avoid further hostilities, leaving Mrs. Fielding to pity herself, and wonder how her children turned out so well, considering what crosses and contradictions she endured.

"It is very sad, Grannie," said Mrs. Cameron, "to see how entirely men of business are absorbed in their occupations in these days. It is worse than living to eat, it is merely living to pay bills. Mr. Cameron returns either too worn out to attend to anything, or if he has any energy left, it relapses into his usual current of calculations."

"It is too true, my dear," said Grannie.

"And then," pursued Mrs. Cameron, "the children are left to their own devices, and spend all their freshest faculties in discovering for themselves what ought to have been their starting-point. Everything is so weighed, and pulled to pieces, and anatomised now, that one is afraid to say the sun shines for fear of being called on to give a definition of light."

"And the worst of this pulling to pieces is," said Grannie gravely, "that

> 'Not the king and all his men
> Can put Humpty Dumpty together again.'"

"These are really most difficult days to live in," replied Mrs. Cameron.

"I believe all times have been difficult to live well in, my dear, since the days of Adam and Eve," replied Grannie.

"But these are too difficult," said Mrs. Cameron, in a tone of petulance unusual with her. "Is it not hard, after all I have said and done, to see Kenneth and Kate wandering one does not know whither? But women cannot do everything, as I told Mr. Cameron the other day."

"Surely, Catharine, you did not say any such thing," exclaimed Grannie (Grannie having very apostolic ideas of the duties of wives). "The nursery is your kingdom, not your husband's."

"What could I have done more?" was the languid reply.

"I am not a mother, dear Catharine, and therefore must speak humbly. The faults and inconsistencies of parents are reflected in children sooner than their virtues and principles. Tricks are caught more easily than graces. It must be a very serious thing to have such accurate magnifying mirrors applied to our lives, and made daguerreotypes of. But single-heartedness, where it exists, is sure in time to have its influence,—with prayer."

"Indeed I have not done half enough, I know," Mrs. Cameron said, in a low appealing voice; "but I have prayed."

"It is not what we do or say so much as what we are, that weighs with all, especially with children. They unconsciously reflect our lives far more then they consciously copy our acts."

"But Grannie, with such a feeling, the responsibility becomes crushing."

"Who doubts that the responsibility is the most solemn on earth!" said Grannie. "God is on your side, my dear, ready to help, and to heal, and to efface."

"Ah," said Mrs. Cameron, "I am afraid there is much to efface in my work. But what could I do, for instance, about this invitation of Lady Fitzroy's? The Fitzroys are so kind. Kate wished to go—I could not remove the wish by denying it. I thought she would learn the emptiness of the world by proving it, as she did not believe me, and she is returned more fascinated with the theatre, the opera, and society than ever;—and yet she is most amiable to me, poor child. What can I do?"

"I know not," replied Grannie, "except pray, and wait, and hope."

"You hope, Grannie?"

"I hope everything," replied Grannie. And just then Kate came in with a huge basket in her hand, for simultaneously with her fit of gaiety had sprung up in her mind a great zeal for visiting the poor and supplying their physical wants, the vacancies left by ball-dresses being supplied by Dorcas frocks and flannel petticoats, which perplexed Mrs. Cameron extremely.

Kate was on her way to Jean's, and there in due time she met her uncle Fielding and Annie.

It was the first mild day after a succession of weather aptly described in almanac style as rain and wind—a languid yet delicious day, which seemed to unite every one in a common feeling of deliverance from the bondage of the weather. The most thrifty shopkeepers stood idly in their shop-doors and nodded to Annie and her father as they went by,—the strokes of the men who were squaring the granite for the new school-rooms at the end of the town, fell in a languid andante,—the stone-breaker on the road anticipated his dinner-time by half an hour, and was sitting in cricketer's costume under the hedge, whilst his dog, stretched in all the animal luxury of repose at his feet, lazily opened one eye to inspect the passers,

—and under garden-walls, on the sunny side of the way, feeble invalids were creeping out to enjoy their first walk.

Mr. More's Vicarage was a "manse" rather than a mansion, not lording it over the heritage on the hill-top, but nestling cosily in the valley, itself one of the village-homes it was meant to bless, old-fashioned, irregular, and low, but very snug and cheerful; with such a garden as only old parsonages have, enriched with the tastes and sweet with the records of generations of cultivated families—a soil to which it has become second nature to bring forth all fragrant common garden flowers. An orchard covered in succession with primroses, sweet violets, blue-bells, and ragged robins—rose-trees, moss, cabbage, and damask, which might have been brought home as a honeymoon gift and sweet rarity by the first Reformed minister in the days of good Queen Bess—old fruit-trees, gray with moss and lichens, old arbors, wild with honeysuckles and periwinkle and jasmine, shaded by a tall old mountain ash, which the gray-haired clerk remembers helping "Master George and Miss Emmy to plant. Poor Master George, he has become a high-learned man at the university since—a deacon, or dean, or something very near a bishop; and Miss Emmy died ten years ago, leaving twenty grandchildren."

Jean was worthy of her home. Everything was so clean, and fresh, and simple, and systematic. You could as easily dissociate the idea of a nautilus from its shell, as of Jean from her little parsonage-house, if you had once seen her there. They seemed one being. The little tables with the appropriate knick-knacks, records of successive birthdays, from childhood upwards—for Jean never broke anything; the shelves with their neat, well-dressed books, from nursery stories onwards—for Jean never tore anything; little worked mats and anti-macassars, and stools and chairs fitting into their places, as if Jean had had prophetic visions of that identical parsonage from her cradle. What a picture and example, as Nurse said, framed and glazed, to all riotous and careless children!

Then the boxes of Dorcas clothes, and the cupboards of preserves, and the books of recipes—when ever was there such a treasurer and secretary of all manner of societies, and such a village doctress, as Jean? Such was Jean's home before any destructive elements made their appearance, or any little hands and feet less conservative than hers intruded into this paradise. But we anticipate.

Kate and Annie rambled in the garden. One or two precocious bees were humming about the early blossoms, and one or two white butterflies, like sainted flowers, hovering and poising noiselessly around their yet earth-bound sisters. Kate had been rehearsing the last opera she had heard to Annie. Annie having been delivered from the sense of constraint, and the painful necessity of perpetual protest, by her last conversation with Grannie, had listened quietly. Kate, however, was not contented with this, and at length she exclaimed—

"But why do I torment you with all this, Annie, when I know you think it all very worldly and heathenish!"

"You do not torment me, dear Kate," said Annie. "I love to hear of all you are interested in."

"As a curious fact in morbid anatomy?"

"How unjust, Kate!"

"Yes, it is not in your nature to be uncharitable, Annie, I do believe. Our theories of life, however, are different; mine is, that enjoyment of God's gifts is one of the most acceptable forms of thanksgiving, and thanksgiving a large part of religion. I hate asceticism."

"So do I," replied Annie.

"Yes, so I believe you all practically do, only every one enjoys in their own peculiar way. Jean's form of thanksgiving is to keep district-books, and put every thing neat, and make chair-coverings—mamma's is to be quiet and kind—aunt Fielding's to be busy—yours to draw etchings, and read divines of the seventeenth century, and to be very dear and good to everybody. Mine is—I have not quite made up my mind what. But I do not think it a sin to rejoice in the beautiful faces and voices God has given to some of His creatures. I think the butterfly fulfils his mission quite as perfectly as the bee, in spite of fables and nursery rhymes; and of the two I think the butterfly's vocation the least groveling and utilitarian, the most spiritual and artistic."

"But we are not butterflies, or bees," rejoined Annie, smiling, "and we do not live in the garden of Eden." The old church clock struck two, and Jean's early dinner was never an instant too late.

The cousins walked home together in the evening, Mr. More accompanying Mr. Fielding.

As they passed Grannie's cottage, Kate said emphatically, after a silence of some duration:

"There, Annie, that is a life I should like to lead, if I were good enough."

"What?" said Annie, who had been pondering her last Greek lesson.

"Grannie's," said Kate. "She is my patron saint. A life really sacrificed to others, and yet it seems unconsciously—every day a fresh, sublime self-consecration, and taking the veil—I cannot imagine a higher vocation. A nun without vows."

"But the process, the training, must have been very trying," replied Annie. "How lonely Grannie must have been between thirty and forty, when youth was gone, and the fire-light and candle-light of her bright old age not begun! I cannot wish for it, Kate."

"Ah, Annie, you are no ascetic," was the laughing reply; "you have satisfied me on that point."

"And yet," said Annie, seriously, "if God

was with her, and she was living from day to day on His strength and in His presence, she could not have been lonely. I spoke unbelievingly, and yet, Kate, I think we cannot wish it. Why cannot we consecrate ourselves to our Father's service now and always? Indeed, if we believe, are we not already consecrated to Him?"

Kate did not reply, and Annie did not at the moment perceive the meaning that lay in this restless oscillation of her cousin's heart between a religion which was to include all that "was in the world," and a religion which was to exclude all natural enjoyment; between a life of the world, and a life not in the world; between a pantheistic deification of Nature, and a monastic renunciation of it. Nor did Kate.

XI.

TRAVELING.

KATE and Kenneth, during his next vacation, had a tour on the continent with an invalid uncle and aunt; and there were letters to Mrs. Cameron full of ecstatic descriptions of rivers and mountains, and Southern skies and Northern cities; and to Annie, scraps of cousinly confidence, which made a charming stir in the smooth current of her life.

"Dearest Annie, there is nothing in the world so delightful as traveling. You must come with us next time; Kenneth says you must. It is eating and drinking and breathing history and all kinds of knowledge. I seem only to have been half awake all my life until now. The very clouds and skies seem to have new colors and forms. The most delicious things are Kenneth and my morning walks, before my aunt and uncle Acton are up, or while they are taking the 'waters,' if there are any to be had, or whatever other medicinal advantages the place may possess. There is one scheme which seems almost too delightful to be realized. It is said they are to remain some weeks at Meyringen for the baths, where the experiment is tried to perfection how far human beings can emulate fish; and as we are satisfied with our present rank in the scale of creation, Kenneth proposes that we should start on a tête-á-tête excursion. It requires some diplomacy to effect this; but we are such exemplary young people, especially since this idea has entered our heads, that I think we may be trusted."

"These glorious, rugged old German cities, as different from the smooth-faced modern ones, as a tailor's ideal of a gentleman from St. Paul's; with expression in every line, and records in every moulding. Everything is so large and linked to universal history here, compared with England. What a strange miniature world England is, Annie, with its own political days and nights, and winters and summers, and systems of storms and currents, as apart from the rest of the earth as if it were a little moon, sailing through space by itself; its revolutions, constitution, philosophers, literature, church, all so separate and so self-contained. I seem to have been stranded in a creek all my life, and now first to be launched on the broad majestic river. What a grand idea this, One Catholic and yet Roman Church, is! its centre so fixed and imperial, its scope so universal, its laws so firm and yet so elastic. Do not alarm aunt Fielding. Of course I only speak as a spectator. You cannot understand Gothic architecture without transforming yourself (only artistically, you understand,) into a 'true believer.' Indeed, I doubt if we can understand or judge any faith without believing it. Religions and churches look so different from within—as Göthe says, somewhere, of poems, They are like painted windows, you look in at them from the market, all is dark and confused, but viewed from inside, all is full of meaning and beautiful forms and colors. But I am in no danger of being seduced by the 'petrified music' of cathedrals, though animated by the soul of the religion at whose wand they rose, or 'dim religious lights,' and sounds, and scents, or any of the manifold enchantments of this worship. Stronger attraction lies in the solitary and sacrificed lives of hundreds—priests and nuns renouncing 'home' for ever (and think of all that home means, Annie), visible prayers and creeds every one of them to me. It is this combination that is so wonderful in this church; the adoption and development in her service of all beauty and joy, art and intellect; and, on the other hand, the voluntary renunciation of all for higher moral aims, by thousands, age after age. It must surely be Divine, or the direct opposite."

"Neither the one nor the other," said Grannie, abruptly, as Annie read this passage; "it is human, thoroughly human; neither Divine nor diabolical; a compound, like Kate and nature, of echoes of Eden with those of the curse."

And some days afterwards:—

"Kenneth and I are among the mountains alone. I am like a child, Annie, I am so happy, and everything gives me such pleasure, earnest pleasure, like a child's, not frivolous, and excited, like men and women trying to live for amusement. These mountains—I think their solemn lights and shadows will be on me all my life, and the great voices that are among them—torrents springing to life, like Adam, full-grown, and yet so free and exulting—winds rushing down chasms, or through the pine forests—and then, higher up, the silence. And yet I feel sure, when I come back to you all, I shall think every flower, and cloud, and old rock and hill more beautiful than ever, from their having such kindred. And the churches, so different from those of the plains, so meek and lowly, pointing upwards, not towering over all, as I suppose we do when we really feel God's presence. Kenneth is making some sketches for you. I am too happy to sketch or do anything."

Then came impressions of the South.

"In the North we may exist, and eat, and grow, and criticise; but here people live. In England the sun lights us to dress, and read, and write; here the sun shines. Every breath seems a thanksgiving. One cannot help feeling God a Father. He has planted such a garden for us. There is nothing ugly here. The beautiful glowing light makes a picture out of every stone and wall. With us Nature sketches and shades very nicely, but here she paints. I think I have never known enjoyment before. I have only been *comfortable.* But it is very ill-natured to give you such disparaging comparisons, dear Annie. Be a good girl; do not envy me, and one day you may enter this paradise yourself, perhaps."

Annie was not the least envious, although Kate's letter arrived on a rainy day, and she had to go out immediately afterwards, with umbrella and clogs, on an expedition to some sick pensioners of her father's; for while Kate and Kenneth were roaming through new worlds, she found her old world ever fresh and new, and was content, twining herself meanwhile by a thousand little loving ministrations round her aunt Cameron's heart, so that when the travelers returned, both Mr. and Mrs. Cameron missed her continually.

"It is very strange, Annie always knew where my spectacles were," said Mrs. Cameron complainingly, an evening or two after Kate's return, "and no one else ever does."

"Annie has the sweetest voice and touch I ever heard," said Mr. Cameron. Kate looked up in amazement. She did not know her father ever listened to music.

Kate was standing musingly the next morning in the library, where Kenneth was reading, when she suddenly soliloquized—

"Annie seems to have a perpetual fountain of freshness within her. I should get a mere machine in that monotonous life of hers, or else make variety by tormenting myself into a tragedy; and she does nothing like a machine, and yet never gets morbid. She goes the same round again and again, and yet it never becomes routine with her. To be sure the sun does the same, and is perpetually coming to fresh mornings; but then he is a 'heavenly body,' as Jean used to teach us."

"This autumn I shall take my degree," was Kenneth's counter-soliloquy. Kate thought him very absent and egotistical.

XII.

RESOLUTIONS.

The next day Kenneth left for Oxford, and the following morning Kate found herself pursuing the train of thought about Annie, in a kind of half-apologetic, half-admonitory strain before she arose.

"May not that very round of uniform occupations be the spring of Annie's freshness and cheerfulness? Does not the very pressure of necessary duties preserve the elasticity of her spirit?"

And Kate's thoughts reverted to the "scheme," and revolved a thousand busy plans, so that she felt as if she had done a day's work before she was dressed, and was rather disposed to resent as an injustice an admonition from her father on her late appearance at breakfast. When breakfast was over, the newspaper finished, Mr. Cameron departed to his business, and Mrs. Cameron standing meditating on hers, Kate went up to her mother with an air of heroic purpose, and said,

"Dear mamma, will you let me take Jean's place, and be your lieutenant-general in the house? I want to be useful."

Mrs. Cameron looked up half absently from her visions of *pieces de resistance* and *rechauffes*, until her eye, happening to rest on her daughter's hurried coiffure, woke into definite perception, and she said,

"My dear child, I have been intending to speak to you about your dress. You really are not particular enough. Even your father noticed it the other day—and you must indeed be down earlier."

Kate was not at all prepared for such a rejoinder, having passed a retrospective act of amnesty with herself that very morning on the strength of what she intended to do, but she humbly received the admonition and returned to her petition.

"I am much obliged to you, dear, but I do not find these little household occupations at all too much for me; I rather enjoy them; and you can, no doubt, find plenty else to do."

And Mrs. Cameron set out for the kitchen.

Thus baffled, Kate took up the first book at hand, and read until the little French clock petulantly announced that it was twelve o'clock, and Mrs. Cameron reappeared, saying,

"I thought you were going to the school this morning, Kate?"

Kate laid down the book, with an indiscriminate condemnation of all book societies, as the great promoters of busy idleness.

"I am sorry you missed the school," resumed Mrs. Cameron.

So was Kate, but she said, "Oh, I dare

say the afternoon will do as well." And then, "It is certainly a great misfortune for me to have been born in the nineteenth century," she exclaimed; "I feel myself a continual anachronism. In the days when Elizabeth Woodville milked her father's cows, I think I might have made a useful member of society."

"My dear," said Mrs. Cameron, unwontedly roused, "I cannot bear to hear you talk so. After all the trouble and expense your father and I have had with your education, it is really very ungrateful. Do go and get your drawing, or something, and not indulge such morbid fancies."

Kate colored, and the tears started to her eyes, and then recovering herself, she laughed good-humoredly, kissed her mother's forehead, and began to inspect her sketch-book for materials of a picture. She was soon engaged, the school was forgotten, and nothing further was thought of until the drawing was finished to her satisfaction. The next morning, when the first love for her work had evaporated, she looked at it with dissatisfied, critical eyes, compared it ocularly with some good modern water-color landscapes on the walls, and mentally with her own canons of criticism and ideal of beauty,—until she was thoroughly displeased with it, and buried it judicially in the recesses of her portfolio, exclaiming, "If I had only one predominant, overwhelming talent, and could do only one thing thoroughly well, better than any one else, so that nature pointed that out as my work; or if there were only one little corner left in the world, which I, and I only, could fill, were it only the corner occupied by the kitchen-maid, I might be happy."

"What nonsense, my dear child," said Mrs. Cameron; "as if you were not necessary to our happiness, and beloved by so many. I really begin to regret I ever urged your father to let you go abroad, you have been so unsettled ever since." Then dread-ing further discussion, and fearing she had been harsh, said, "Do you not intend to visit the school this morning? You have only an hour left."

Kate dressed and went; but in the spirit which possessed her that morning, she was not likely to do or get much good. On her way home she met Grannie.

"Where are you coming from?"

"From the Infant School."

Grannie looked pleased. "I am glad you are interesting yourself in the children."

"I do not know that I am," replied Kate; "I do not know that I am really interested in anything. The children seemed very busy, and in very good order, every one seemed to have something to do except me, and no one seemed to want me; so after interrupting them for a few minutes, I came away."

"You will get more at home there by and by."

A silence.

"I wish," said Kate, at length, "I were

either young enough to be set tasks to, or else had genius."

"Rather different alternatives," remarked Grannie.

"How happy men of genius must be, Grannie!"

"Why?" said Grannie. "One would not think so from their lives."

"It must be so happy," continued Kate, "to have some one master-taste, or gift, or work."

"Will not one master-feeling do as well, Kate? Women are not made, commonly, with one predominant gift, nor for one predominant pursuit, but to pick up fragments and fill up corners here and there. We are, I think, rather set to be gleaners than reapers in the great harvest. To the end we are to be the help-meets."

"Yes, that is the great privilege of men, to have a profession—to have a grand unity in their lives. It is very sad to be nothing but mortar all one's life, Grannie."

"True, my child, the great danger we are exposed to is to fritter away our lives. But there is one thing which can give to woman's life a unity quite as perfect as that of man. If we cannot have unity of object, we can have unity of feeling; unity of motive, Kate, will bind our scattered fragments of work and thought together in perfect harmony; and motives have their birth-place in the heart."

"Yes; but where can we find the standing-point for this lever which is to stir our world?"

"Not *in* our world, certainly," was Grannie's answer.

"It is object, aim, a sufficient motive for exertion, that I want," Kate rejoined; "as long as I had the day filled with school-hours and play-hours, I was happy, and I should no doubt have been happy if I had been the elder sister of ten children, or a dairymaid, or a genius, or anything which leaves me no time to ask, What good is there in all I am doing? Who will benefit by it?"

"My child, I can only repeat, it is not object, but motive, that you want; not a world to move, but a point from which to move it; not some end to aim at, but a feeling, a motive to work from."

"True, Kenneth says, work is itself the end of work. I suppose it was the motive, not the result, which inspired St. Teresa and Mrs. Fry, but I am neither. There are no Orders to be reformed in these Protestant days, and I have not that passion of benevolence which assigns a life's work as distinctly as genius."

"Kate," said Grannie, abruptly and very earnestly, "when will you be tired of playing with truth, and treating your soul as if it were a biography of some one else, to be anatomized and coolly dissected?"

"Indeed, Grannie," replied Kate, her voice faltering with the tears her pride checked, "every one seems unjust to me to-day; I never felt less disposed to play, or to take things coolly. I am not at all happy."

"I have fancied that long, Kate."

"Kenneth says it is a miserable selfishness," she replied, "to be seeking happiness; that it is not the end of life to enjoy, but to do nobly and endure bravely, and take up and off from others, if it may be, some portion of the sorrow under which this poor world groans; but I am not strong enough for this."

"Kenneth is right in a great measure," replied Grannie; "peace is not the end of life, but its beginning. To serve and rescue others, you must yourself be free. My child, you and Kenneth will never grind a grain of food for your souls out of all your theories, except by chance some stray grains have fallen between your millstones from the old granary. You need the gospel, Kate."

"I need something to make myself complete, certainly," replied Kate, "for I am a very faulty, and imperfect, and ineffectual instrument as it is."

"You are not only faulty and incomplete, dear Kate," replied Grannie; "you are sinful and lost."

Kate shrank and started; the words seemed so harsh, and yet the tone was so inexpressibly gentle and tender, she could not reply except in words that belied the earnestness of her heart.

"That is little consolation, Grannie."

"Yet there is no consolation that is not grounded on it. Our Lord, dearest Kate, did not come merely to guide those who were perplexed, he came to save those who were lost. He did not come to mend—but to create. I cannot talk more to you now, but go home, I entreat you, and pray to be taught what our Lord meant, when he met an intelligent, and thoughtful, and earnest-minded man, coming to him for instruction and guidance, with the overwhelming declaration, 'Ye must be born again.' Learn the awful necessity, dear Kate, and you will surely also prove the blessed possibility. You have occupied yourself much with your *faults*, have you ever humbled yourself because of your *sins?*"

XIII.

STORMS, CONFLICTS, AND COUNSELINGS.

THE usual evening avocations were performed by Kate that evening, at least by Kate's eyes and lips, reading to her father and mother, and her fingers playing to them in the twilight. But her spirit was in none of these things; it was possessed by Grannie's words; and the first hour she was alone, the Bible was taken out for such a search as she had never given it before. Gradually, however, theological controversies and conflicting theories about the sacred words, the ghosts of past readings and conversations, arose like evil spirits around her, blinding her heart with their misty forms, and deafening it by their thousand voices of doubt, or mockery, or eloquent error. She would have given anything to have made a silence in her heart, but she could not—and at length, closing the volume impatiently, she said a few words of wandering prayer, and settled herself to sleep with a mind as empty as before of light, but full of subtle and puzzling questions, with which she determined to assault Grannie on the morrow.

Accordingly, at the next interview, she met Grannie with sundry serious whats and perplexing hows.—Was there not a basis of pure humanity in every heart on which to build? Did not some people think regeneration was merely the development of this germ? What became of personal identity, if the new nature had no link with the old? What became of personal responsibility, if before this new birth we are absolutely dead? And then there were so many different theories and opinions as to the time and signs of the imparting of this new life. The Bishop of Exeter, the Bishop of Oxford, Mr. Gorham, Archdeacon Hare, not to mention others who fell below or shot above the utmost limits of Anglican orthodoxy—what did Grannie think of all these various shades?

To all this Grannie replied very little—and Kate thought her rather cool and uninterested, until looking up she saw tears in her eyes, and an expression of the gentlest love and pity. She was silent for some moments, and then Grannie said,

"Dear Kate, I thought your soul was hungering for living bread, and I see you only want a lesson on theological confectionery."

Kate colored, half in anger, half in pain, and then a few tears forced their way under her downcast eyelids.

Grannie continued: "To those who want to know how to be forgiven and saved, the Bible is, as you would imagine from its Author it would be, the plainest book in the world. To those who come to make from it theories about salvation and the universe, I believe it is at once the most impenetrable and the most accommodating book ever written. Now, which do you want?"

Kate's tears flowed now, no longer checked; but she could not reply.

"Dear Kate," Grannie went on, gently taking her hand, "there is nothing but pride which can be a barrier between you and your Saviour. Conscious sin is no barrier between the sinner and Him who bears sin away—conscious weakness is no hindrance in approaching Him who came to heal the sick. There is nothing, nothing but pride which can keep off your soul from God and peace."

"Oh, Grannie," Kate murmured, "indeed I have nothing to be proud of."

"I do not think you have ever felt," Grannie continued, "what *sin* is. I am sure you cannot, or you would be too anxious to get it blotted out, and to be forgiven, to have time for theorizing about it. Shipwrecked men have no heart to listen to acute.

essays on the best construction of lifeboats. You know, of course, that you have done many things you ought not to have done, and left undone many things you ought to have done—but have you ever really felt and confessed that 'there is *no health in you?*' You know you have many faults—but have you ever seriously perceived and acknowledged, in the depths of your heart, that you yourself are essentially *sinful?* You have felt uneasy, restless, dissatisfied, my child—but have you ever felt *guilty?*"

The silence was made at length in Kate's heart, and she felt, instead of that restless desire to consult every one, and try every source of peace and light, the necessity of being alone with God.

Many conflicts and fluctuations followed. The Bible became a new book to her, not by any new intellectual discoveries she made in it, but from the simple fact of her reading it no more as a mere collection of histories and religious biographies and essays on Christian doctrine by inspired men, but as a dialogue between God and her inmost soul; God in heaven, her soul humbled in the dust. Every page became instinct with life—every verse laden with the most solemn messages. She learned that it is in the silence God speaks—that it is the poor and empty heart he fills. She learned that humility is not in lost and fallen creatures what it may be in holy and angelic creatures, a joyful prostration of the heart, and reverent vailing of the face before the Mightiest and Holiest, the Creator of all; but a trembling perception of what we are and were—an awakening to the reality of our degradation and fall; not so much a *virtue* as a *sense*—not a bending downwards as angels may from the battlements of heaven, but a looking upwards from the dust; not so much the ornament of the believing soul, as its essence. She learned what it means to be poor in spirit—yet at first she did not receive the blessing annexed. She felt she had been so proud, so full of self, and that she was so still.

She longed to empty her heart of all its pride and selfishness—but she could not. Her gaze seemed fascinated there, and she could not look upwards and see the Sun, although it was shining full upon her, and revealing to her the dark chambers amongst which she wandered solitary and mourned.

And meanwhile she pursued her usual occupations—wrote letters, answered invitations, paid morning calls, went out to dinner, did Berlin wool-work, drew, and played, and sang. The sun and the moon do not stand still in these days, when the armies of God and the evil one are engaged.

And no one, even of those who watched her so tenderly and anxiously, knew what was passing in Kate's spirit. Such impenetrable invisible garments hide our souls from one another. Even Annie, who had offered, and continually offered, so many prayers for her cousin, knew not in the least that God was answering them. Often, indeed, her faith was sorely tried, and it seemed as if something hindered her prayers from ascending, or God's blessing from coming down. So silently did the dew fall, and the blossom open. Is it not often so with us?—our despondency is deepest when help is nearest. We seem forgotten, and all the while God is bowing down His ear and listening, and He who has entered within the veil for us is pleading, and the angels are rejoicing, and the Spirit descending, and the soul swelling into life.

Only the mother's eye traced some indescribable change in her child. A softened demeanor, a gentler tone, a something subdued and quiet, broken indeed at times by intervals of more than usual impatience and impetuosity; yet Mrs. Cameron fancied—she scarcely dared to hope—these were indications of a heart awakened and watching itself. And one evening, coming unexpectedly into the school-room, she saw Kate bending over the Bible with tears on her cheeks. Softly she closed the door again. Had she waited, perhaps Kate might have fallen on her mother's heart, and told all that was struggling within. But she did not, and perhaps it is better to be left alone in such conflicts, to prove our utter weakness, that we may learn to rest more entirely on His strength.

XIV.

TWILIGHT.

If all true history may be said to be the essence of biographies, true ecclesiastical history is so more than all. We speak of mornings, and mid-days, and evenings among the ages, and doubtless some truth lies under the figure. We, being short-sighted, and having limited memories, are compelled to generalize, and condense biographies into history, for the convenience of traveling through this busy and hurried world. But that book of universal biography which is daily being written in heaven is, we may be sure, no philosophical abstraction of history, no mere record of successive phases of opinion and principle, but a collection of Lives of the Saints. Perhaps one of the most difficult things for us to believe, and the most impossible for us to conceive, is the individuality of God's dealings with men. God does not need the aid of classifications. Every soul stands before Him as individual and distinct as Adam's did when he first looked forth alone on the world. With every soul He acts as individually as He did with Adam when His voice was heard at noon in the silent garden calling him. Every soul has its history, and in many how strangely the religious history of the world is re-enacted! Eden, the natural rejoicing in creation; the law, the gospel; dispensation after dispensation; the "early days of faith and love," the middle ages, with their darkness and quaintly-colored illuminations, the Reformation, the era of skepticism; primitive ages, dark ages, and cold ages; era after era; how they are repeated unconsciously in the soul, some pausing at one step, some at another. So many centuries are contemporary in one. Every hour of the day exists at once every day in our world.

Toujours un astre a son réveil,
Partout où s'abaisse Ta vue
Un soleil levant Te salue.

It was this individuality, this being alone with God, that Kate was now experiencing. And this was much. A kind of unacknowledged Pantheism is so natural to us, a representation of God as a Thought * rather than a Person, an ethereal Essence, an Ocean of Life, Infinity, Deity, anything rather than *God.* She was learning the reality of things unseen. Her soul was awake, and she stood not rejoicing but trembling. Her soul was awake, but her eyes were not yet fully unveiled. She was conscious of the personal presence of God, but she was not conscious of a personal relationship to Him; and at the same time she was convinced of sin;—the most awful combination that can exist in the human soul. With Kate, enough of the general recognition of Redemption existed to prevent this double consciousness from be-

* Lebendig der höchste Gedanke.—*Schiller.*

coming the overwhelming and distracting thought it has been with some intense and strong hearts from St. Paul downwards, although not enough to reconcile these contradictions, and bring light and order into her soul. Not that Kate was by any means conscious of all this; had she been so she would at once have had the clue. We cannot feel and analyze at the same moment. No soldier fighting in the thick of the battle can see the plan of the battle. That may be seen from the heights; or learned from the relics and trophies afterwards; but at the time it is blood, and fire, and vapor of smoke, and passion and pain—and that is all. And this is one reason why Christians can do so much for one another, and the weakest often help the strongest. We are not all at the same stage of our pilgrimage at once; one is on the Shepherds' Mountains, telling the towers of the "City," whilst another is in the depths of the Valley of Humiliation; one is resting whilst another is in the conflict;

one is being refreshed whilst another is being tried. And thus it is that the least are not shut out from service, and the hand of a child may bring a cordial to the heart of a veteran.

Something of this kind Annie said to Kate one morning, when, after bemoaning her selfishness, she appealed to her for advice and help, as so infinitely above herself in love and faith and everything.

"Dearest Kate, we do not give of our own to help one another, or if we do, it would be of little use—we can only open God's treasury."

"I would give anything, Annie, to love God as you do."

Annie looked up in amazement. It seemed so often as if she scarcely loved Him at all—and she said so.

"I suppose St. John might have felt that," Kate replied; "yet, Annie, you could answer with St. Peter, 'Lord, Thou knowest that I love Thee.'"

Annie looked up with tears in her eyes. She felt she could.

"But Annie, I cannot," Kate continued, in a tone almost of anguish, "it seems as if I could not love anything but myself."

"Dear Kate," said Annie, rising from her drawing and kneeling beside her cousin, "Have you ever thought that God really loves you?—that our Lord really died because He so loved us, because there was no other way to save us?"

"A thousand times," said Kate seriously, yet with some bitterness, "but my heart is as cold as ever."

"But do you really believe it, Kate?"

The question in the old spirit of acting riddles, "What is faith?" was on Kate's lips, but she did not utter it. She said gently, "Pray for me, dear Annie," and turned the conversation.

Yet Annie's words, although they seemed to Annie so feeble, and although Kate seemed little to regard them, were among the thousand influences which worked together at that time, under God, to bring Kate's heart into light and peace; perhaps, however, much more Annie's prayers. But the links which bind prayers to blessings are invisible.

An east wind had been blowing for weeks, blowing from Siberia across the steppes of Russia, the plains of Northern Germany, and the flat manufactured fields of Holland, laden with the quintessence of sighs and groans and grumblings, from Polish exiles, and Prussian democrats, and English malcontents; a rough, hard, dry, lifeless wind, without a civil word to say to any one. The blossoms opened as if they had grown old and shriveled in the bud; every clod of earth seemed bent on claiming an individual existence for itself distinct from every other clod; the flower-seeds rotted in the ground; the birds of that season handed down to their posterity very confused and limited notions of spring. The very clouds in the sky seemed of dust rather than of water; as if there had been fans on Olympus.

Grannie and Kate sat on the old seat under the garden-wall, and looked over the terraced garden.

"Grannie," said Kate, "it seems sometimes as if an east wind were blowing over my heart, and nothing will grow or look fresh there."

"The heart is watered, like Egypt, from a stream within it, a river that flows from the mountains and is never dry."

"I know it, Grannie. I want life—living waters within. I want them; and that is all I know."

"'If thou hadst asked of me,'" repeated Grannie, "'I would have given thee living water:' then, dearest Kate, you would no more need to come hither to this world again and again to draw."

"Kenneth would say it is weakness and rebellion to look for peace and joy, Grannie;

that patience and earnest activity are all the brave heart will seek; but I do not think the Bible says so."

"You do not *think*, dear child? What was our Lord's last promise, what was His last legacy? What shines at the head of every Epistle?—and the apostles did not deal in compliments. Peace, peace. Grace and peace abounding, multiplied; peace always, by all means. Peace in Jesus. Peace with God. Peace keeping the heart, not as its guest, but its garrison, dwelling in its citadel."

"But is it not the great end of the gospel to set us free from selfishness?"

"Indeed, I believe, it is. But God does not free us from selfishness by precepts, but by gifts. He gives us freely more than heart can desire, or conceive; breaks the fetters, opens the prison, pays the debt, makes us children and heirs, and then says, Love me, and labor for others. He destroys the great void in the heart by filling it."

"But for *me*, Grannie; how can this peace, these gifts, become mine?"

"By believing in Jesus," replied Grannie, solemnly.

"But how am I to believe, Grannie? I know faith is the root of every good—but how am I to believe?"

Grannie paused some moments, and then said,

"Do you *not* believe, Kate?"

"How can I," Kate answered, very sadly, "when all these blessed things you speak of —peace, and love, and all—flow from faith, and I have none of them?"

"There are a thousand ways of being wrong," Grannie said, "and only one of being right; and God forbid that I should tempt you to mistake a dead belief for a living faith. I cannot see your heart, my dearest child, but from your words I cannot but think that you are mistaking the nature of faith, and attributing a kind of saving virtue to it, instead of to Christ—looking within for your Saviour, instead of above. This difficulty seems anticipated in the Bible. In one place we have, *Believe* and be saved; in another, *Look* and be saved; in another, *Come* unto me: as if to draw our attention from the act, which is nothing, to the object, which is everything. The definition in the Hebrews teaches us the same. Faith is the substance of things hoped for, the evidence of things not seen. Then it is the substance of things hoped for, the evidence of things not seen, which saves us. The essence of faith, as of love, is self-forgetfulness. Are you thoroughly dissatisfied with yourself, Kate; thoroughly convinced that you are indeed sinful and lost, and have nothing worthy to offer God?"

"I see nothing—not even real sorrow for sin, real self-abhorrence, not even tears."

"Then look away from yourself, from your sins, your weakness, your wants, and look at Christ leaving heaven for you, becoming man for you, made a curse for you, dying on the cross, despised, forsaken of God, yet without sin; all for you."

"For *me*, Grannie?" said Kate, her voice faltering.

"For all sinners," replied Grannie; "the message, the promise is to *sinners*, to all, to each; no limitation, no reservation. Not to those who have loved, or those who have repented, or those who have wept for their sins, but simply to those who have *sinned*."

Kate did not speak.

"And then," pursued Grannie, her old thin voice growing full and strong with emotion as she spoke, "look at Him, saying 'It is finished'—rising from the dead, appearing alone to Mary as she wept for Him—breathing peace on the disciples, entering into the Holiest, the Lamb of God, and now the Priest entering there with His own blood, having made atonement for us; and there still, there at this moment, pleading for us—Himself the accepted Sacrifice, the Plea which can never fail. My child, look at

Him, and can you distrust, can you *not* believe? Is not what I have been telling you true?"

Still Kate did not speak. But she wept. The east wind had passed from her heart. And hastily leaving Grannie, she sought once more to be alone.

The conviction of sin had broken her heart, and now the tidings of redemption had melted it. She did not think, nor reason, nor analyze. Her whole heart seemed turned into an organ of sight; and the object which filled it was our Redeemer.

She had found the Sacrifice which could expiate sin; she had found the Priest who can absolve; she had found One who would link her soul to God. If before the Bible had become her most earnest study, now it became her dearest treasure. Before, she had read it as the solemn voice of God to her soul, but now she read it also as the gracious voice of her Father to His child. What was the source of this? What is conversion?

The simplest thing in the world. She believed that God was true, and trusted to His word.

The hardest thing in the world. God had created her soul anew.

XV.

DAYLIGHT AND ITS WORK.

FRANK and communicative as Kate's disposition was, she could not speak much of this new joy. It so pervaded all things, was so new and yet so natural, so changed her relation to everything without changing the outward aspect of anything; it was so sacred and yet so simple, so satisfied every desire of her heart, and yet so raised her above herself, that she could not describe her feelings to any one, and yet every act and word uttered them to those who watched her. It was so different from all her former resolutions and reformations; she had no grand scheme of new activities, she had no restless desire to multiply probability into certainty, by getting others to agree with her, or to buoy her faint purpose up by sympathy. Her mind had found a substance, a rock to rest on; her heart was full, her whole being was at rest, and was quiet; and although it did indeed often break forth into singing, it was mostly to God when alone. Every new human relationship which God gives us opens a sealed fountain of love in the heart. And this new conscious relationship of hers to God embraced and surpassed all the various kinds of human love, of which it is the source and primeval type. It opened her whole heart, "all the fountains of the deep and the windows of heaven" at once, and overflowed it all with deep, satisfied love, deepening, like a flood, all the old channels, and filling them afresh. In this God's religion differs from any invented by men: theirs begin by drying up the old channels to feed some new one; His fills the old channels first, deepening and widening them, and only then creates new courses. Old duties became so sacred to Kate, old truths so fresh, old love so inexpressibly tender. She felt to her mother as she used when a child, or as if they had been separated for years, and had only met again yesterday—the love, the care, the prayers, the anxieties of years, seemed now first to become known to her, and often filled her heart to bursting with the longing, not to repay—love does not keep accounts—but to show how she understood—felt it all. And even little forgotten kindnesses of aunt Fielding's came over her with a gush of tenderness. Her being near God, brought her nearer all His creatures. Mr. More's rather dry and theological sermons touched her heart, as if they had been the most eloquent appeals that ever stirred the hearts of the hearers of apostles — to her they were eloquent, and she quite wondered the next Sunday, when on coming out of church, her father said,

"Your brother was certainly very rambling to-day. I could not make out any connection or arrangement whatever in his sermon."

The sermon had seemed to her the most beautiful she had ever heard: it had spoken so much of Christ, and brought her so immediately into the presence of God. She had been transformed from a critic into a worshiper. If streams were to write a history of vegetation, would they not say it was always fresh and green? And then when alone in the garden and the woods, how full and peopled the solitude was! She had no visions of angels, her eyes were not opened to see the horsemen of Israel and the chariots thereof; nor did she need such revelations. One Presence filled and flooded the world with light and joy; the presence of its Maker, and Her Father, reconciled to her by the infinite sacrifice of her Saviour. What joy there was for her in tracing His present working in all around; "joys that did often lie too deep for tears," in the mere sense that His hand was opening every blossom around her, and guiding every star; joy, and thrilling awe at times, as if she had found her way alone into some solitary sanctuary, with the Glory abiding there. Every day seemed like a birth-day, a beginning of new vistas of time—and the beauty of the common things in the garden and fields as she opened her window in the morning, the air and sunshine, and the old everyday blessings of her home, seemed as if they were new-year's gifts laid for the first time on her table. Was it only *seemed?* Does not God spread our table fresh every day? are not all His gifts daily gifts?—"a continual allowance given us of the King—a daily rate for every day all the days of our life."

She began to rise early. It was worth while. There was so much to learn, so much to enjoy. She so desired to know God's whole will concerning her, and to be subject to Him in all things; and the time seemed so short.

One morning she had wandered out into the garden before breakfast with her Bible.

Her mother came out from the dining-room and joined her.

"How beautiful everything is, mother! I seem to have been living in an ice-palace, under the full current of life until now, and now first to be floating on its waves and feeling what the sunshine really is—sunshine which warms and ripens as well as lights."

"You seem very happy, Kate," said Mrs. Cameron, gently taking her hand.

"Ah, mother," said Kate, smiling, while her voice quivered, "you will not believe any more of my resolutions and grand projects of being good and useful, and I do not mean to make any."

"You are right, Kate—God gives strength for the day."

"Yet," rejoined Kate, "I have one thing to ask. Will you read the Bible with me every morning?"

They understood each other. Had the mother heard that she was to lose her child before the year was gone, I think it would hardly have ruffled the deep joy of that moment.

And when Annie came next to spend a day at Eastwood, and after their usual walk they were hesitating what book to read, Kate said, half timidly,

"Would you like to read the Bible, Annie?"

And she brought one, and they sat together in the garden and read, as they had done with their story-books when they were children.

"Shall we pray before we read?" said Kate softly.

The tears fell fast from Annie's eyes as she asked, in a few simple broken words, that He who wrote that blessed Book for them would teach it to them. And hand in hand they read as when they were children, and spoke of their Father's house, and of Him who was preparing it for them, and of Annie's own mother, who had gone to be with Him—it seemed so near—until evening fell on the world, with its calm, but could add no calm to their hearts. They read St. John's records of the love of God, and Kate whispered, "Annie, I believe it now."

"O Grannie, what is wanted but God's presence," said Kate, "to make the world an Eden again?" as they met Grannie coming to send them in out of the night air; and separating they each claimed a hand of hers. Grannie looked tenderly on them: she saw that what Kate took for a haven was but a bark,—but she could not bear to cast a shadow on her heart; so she said,

"The presence of our Father does indeed make it Eden in the heart, dear children. By and by it will be Eden in the world too."

A few days afterwards an invitation came for Kate from the Fitzroys to accompany them to a county ball. She smiled, and showed the letter to her mother.

"Do you wish to go, my dear?"

"Dear mother, what do I want of such

amusements now? My heart would not be at all in harmony with them."

"Not even as your form of thanksgiving, Kate?" said Annie, rather maliciously, looking up from her work.

"It would not be enjoyment to me," was her reply, "and therefore it would not be thanksgiving. My only regret is that I do not like to do anything unkind to the Fitzroys. How can I convince them that it is because I *have* better joys, and not in the ascetic endeavor to earn them, that I have ceased to care for these things?"

"You cannot convince them," replied Mrs. Cameron; "and if you could, you would only persuade them to become ascetics."

"I can only go straight forward then," replied Kate, "and leave the result." And she wrote an apology.

"What a pity!" said Adelaide Fitzroy, as she threw down Kate's answer; "I suppose it is true, then, that Kate Cameron has become Evangelical."

"I always thought her an enthusiastic girl," remarked her mother, "and it is in the family, I believe."

A few days afterwards Kate wrote a letter from her inmost heart to Kenneth.

He read it rather impatiently, and then said to himself, "My dear, impulsive, imaginative little sister! So Kate has gone through the whole orthodox process at last! Well, it is a wonder she escaped so long."

But in that inner region which is beyond that of "sayings" even to ourselves, what strange vibrations, and echoes of old longings and convictions, were aroused by those simple words of his sister's, and mingled with his outer thoughts and words in eddies of discord?

And could Kate have heard these and a thousand other such comments, how empty they would have been to her!—they could not have penetrated to that citadel of her heart, kept as it was by peace.

Gigantic strides, it may be thought, to

have made in a few weeks. But must not the passage from death to life ever be a gigantic stride? Must not creation always be a sudden act, whether suddenly perceived or not? One moment light was not, the next, light was,—one moment the eye was blind, the next, it saw. The conversion of the soul is not the rising of a sun that had set for a while, but the new creation of light. Although in the change from chaos to Eden there may be a thousand eras and a thousand stages, creation is one act; there is no gradual transition between something and nothing; there are no links which bind together life and death. The consciousness of this marvellous change may not, indeed, be always as sudden, nor is its commencement limited to any stage of the subsequent progress; but whether it be at the first dim and perplexing perception of men as trees walking, or not until each delicate beauty of form and color has revealed itself to the eye, that the delicious consciousness of recovered sight flows in on the soul, surely there must be great lack of thankfulness in any on whom the wondrous miracle has been wrought, if they cannot in prostrate adoration at the feet of the Healer say, whether in a whisper or a song of praise, "Whereas I was blind, now I see."

An infinite step, indeed,—and yet Kate was but a little child in the heavenly family, —although even to the little children it is given to know the Father.

At first it seemed to Kate as if there could be no difficulties or sorrows more. In the first solemn sense of entrance into a world of realities, and realities so joyful,—in the first glow of confidence in the living God, in the first blessed consciousness of being sustained by an Almighty arm,—all things that could oppose themselves seemed so dwarfish, so petty, that, comparing the forces of the enemy, not with her own, but with those of God, it seemed as if the whole warfare would be one triumphal Progress and entry into the Holy City. She had to learn that though life *might*, to the believing, be indeed a perpetual victory, it is also a perpetual and most real battle,—with real weariness and faintness, and real wounds piercing the soul even when they least subdue it. She had to learn much of that deadliest enemy, bound up with every fibre of her heart, with an inexhaustible fertility of stratagem and an unwearying watchfulness and strength—*her own evil nature;* she had to learn, not indeed theologically, but practically, that her own heart, although the Holy Spirit deigned to dwell there, was for her no inviolate sanctuary, but itself a battle-field, and the most perilous of all.

For the rest, I am not drawing a model, but making a sketch, not attempting to say what every one ought to feel, but what Kate felt. The features of every landscape are as varied as the materials are similar.

Kate's first disappointment was from Kenneth. Eagerly she devoured his answer, hoping to find some silent string touched by her letter, some longing for the Gift she had embraced, or at least some opposition or criticism betraying a secret restlessness or uneasiness, and the existence of a felt though unacknowledged want. But there was nothing of the kind—nothing could be kinder or more brotherly, the most minute pieces of news in her letter were commented on, but not an allusion to the subject of which it was full; and Kate wept bitter tears of mortification and grief. She confided her disappointment to her mother.

"My child," was her quiet reply, "we have watched, and watered, and waited for years, and you are in despair because your harvest does not ripen with one shower."

Kate thought of the first crop of cress she had sown to surprise her mamma on her birth-day, what an age the week which ripened it had seemed, how she had mistrusted the gardener, and suspected the birds, and fancied the whole course of nature must have been interrupted to the disadvantage of her particular patch of cress, and how, nevertheless, precisely on the birth-day it was ready; and she smiled through her tears.

"I am a mere child, dear mother, in faith and patience, yet."

She wrote other letters, affectionate, gentle, persuasive; she sent Kenneth books, but still he said nothing, except the most cursory thanks for her kind present, or congratulations on the happiness she seemed to be enjoying, or general acknowledgments of the necessity of being in earnest; and at length she felt she could only watch and wait, and be ready to pour in supplies as soon as the communication was open.

Very soon the desire of doing good to others became a constraining feeling in Kate's heart. She felt she had a blessed secret to tell, and it seemed as if every one must believe it. It no longer felt strange to her to be in the cottages and the schools, and by the bedside of the sick. She longed to be permitted to serve her heavenly Master; not, as of old, from a vague desire of being good, but because it was His command; there was all the difference between submission to a law, and loyalty to a sovereign. The law was bound around her heart by love.

And service always, more or less, brings trial, being thus "twice blessed," disciplining whilst it enriches, for no blossom or fruit in God's garden is lost; the fallen flower enriches the soil as the gathered fruit does the garner.

And doubtless Kate's difficulties were not a little caused by her own mistakes. But Grannie said she would rather see any one who was speaking of important truths in a new language, earnest enough to make a thousand blunders, than so cool as never to forget a termination in a thought.

Mrs. Fielding was still a little suspicious and afraid of Kate. She extremely dreaded enthusiasm, and she had no great faith in sudden changes, and she had a great horror of puffing up young people; and she replied to Kate's meek demand for a class in the Sunday-school by saying:

"Certainly, my dear; I wished you to undertake one years ago."

"But, dear aunt, I could not have taught the children then what I long to teach them now."

"I am not going to discourage you, my dear, but you must not expect great results; and you must be careful not to excite the children's feelings, and not to mistake a few childish tears, or a little emotion, for a real and permanent work. I have known the most promising turn out the worst."

Kate tried not to feel discouraged, although her heart sank to a very low level; but she was struck with the contrast of these words with Grannie's.

"Expect much blessing, my child; pray for much and expect much. Remember, I do not say, expect *to see* much. And do not forget that you are laboring, not only for human beings who may and will often fail and disappoint you, but chiefly for the love of Him who *never* fails or disappoints. Hope becomes as sure and firm a thing as faith when it is fed by His promises."

And with a cheerful trust, Kate began her labors with her class. She sought them out at their homes, she studied for them, she tried to make the physical geography of Palestine and the customs of old times vivid and real things to them. She sought to bring all she had seen and learned under tribute to them, until Mrs. Fielding begged she would not attempt to make the children conceited, by a smattering of all sorts of things. She bought prize-books for them, until she found that this distinction raised an insurrectionary spirit among the less-favored scholars, and occasioned whispers about something like "class-legislation;" but above all, she prayed with them. She learned lessons of thankfulness from a smile of intelligence, and new interest about heavenly things awakened in

KATE VISITING THE POOR.

Two Vocations. p. 206.

some dull or clouded face; from tears occasionally softening hearts which had seemed too light and sandy for any impression, or to retain what was poured into them; she learned lessons of her own weakness from her frequent failures, her coldness in speaking of what lay deepest in her heart, the indifference often shown to tidings of the most overpowering love; she learned patience and experience and hope both from dark and bright hours.

One of her great joys was the new living bond of sympathy which united her to the Christian poor. In all the first and deepest feelings of our nature, they had, indeed, been ever of one race; but once beyond the family records and the details of pain and want, with all the wide barriers of education and position, the experience of life so different, the subjects which occupied the thoughts so wide apart, often it had seemed like preaching in a foreign language, when she tried to address them, but now a wide common field was opened for them. In the highest things which can occupy the thoughts of the wisest they could understand one another. In that region which lies so infinitely beyond the changing fashions of worldly philosophy and literature they were equal. The book they loved best was the same, their hopes and eternal dwelling-place were the same, their family interests were the same—they had become kindred. Yet here also there were necessarily many discouragements: dying people who valued the jelly or the coals infinitely beyond all the messages of Divine love and all the offers of heavenly bliss; hearts that seemed too dull to penetrate; earnest appeals answered by lifeless assent; or worse still, believers in the unspeakable gift of God, who would often appear to think their aches and pains heavier than all the glory that should be revealed in them. But Kate looked within and learned to forbear, and looked above and learned to hope.

But to no one were Kate's feelings more

deepened than to her father. Mr. Cameron was one of those men with whom feeling only comes to the surface at rare intervals, when the whole being is shaken by some convulsion. He had, indeed, petted and caressed all his children with the most indulgent fondness when they were babies and playthings, and Kate, as the youngest, had been his pet and plaything all her life; but now Kate began to feel that this was not enough, and she wondered often to think how close their two hearts had been all her life, close and knit around each other, and yet such hidden worlds to one another; so close, and yet so closed as regarded each deeper thought and feeling. She looked at the new scent-bottle Kenneth had brought from Oxford for her mother, formed of two glass horns intertwined, each containing a different scent, and it seemed the very symbol of the relationship between her and her father, intertwining but never mingling. The barrier seemed the more impenetrable from being transparent. It seemed what glass windows must seem to those baffled bees who buzz so indignantly against them; not so much a barrier as a spell. And she sometimes thought her mother felt the same. Mr. Cameron was not morose, nor his wife unsympathizing, but gradually two different worlds had grown up around them; and though neither was excluded from the creation of the other, each came there not as an inhabitant, but as a guest. Mrs. Cameron heard occasionally of certain great schemes in business, and felt occasionally the result in having to dismiss a servant or to add a luxury, but to the plans and anxieties which filled her husband's head with ceaseless calculations and his brow with wrinkles, she was a stranger. She would have been as much at home in a sum in logarithms. And Mr. Cameron dined and breakfasted and slept, and was entertained in his own house, but knew as little of what was passing in the heads or hearts of any member of his family, beyond such thoughts and feelings as occasionally sprang to the surface, as he knew of the interior of Undine's palace under the Mediterranean.

Mrs. Cameron had grown used to this, but Kate awaking to it now for the first time, with her greater energy of will, and greater ignorance of difficulties, felt it very unnatural and painful.

She hailed most gladly, therefore, an invitation of her father's to ride with him sometimes before breakfast. She endeavored to speak naturally to him of what lay deepest in her own mind and heart, and only felt, from the effort it cost, how far apart they had hitherto lived. She could not get very far, and she scarcely knew how far her father understood her; but she found him not unfrequently reading the books she had spoken of, and he seemed clearly to perceive that some great change had come over Kate,—a change which, whatever his opinion as to its cause, increased the playful tenderness of his manner towards her, and his apparent interest in all she did.

To her mother the subject was never broached.

Must the vessels be in some way shattered and broken before the three perfumes could be poured forth and mingle?—The thought came at times across Kate's imagination, and made her tremble.

XVI.

A DECISION.

KENNETH came back from his last term at college. His manner was so gentle to every one, that Kate could not help at times hoping more from his conversation than from his letters. It was with strangely changed and mingled feelings that she welcomed him. Tenfold deeper was the love she felt for him, and yet between them had grown up a barrier which she felt to be indeed real. If confidence had been difficult in their correspondence, it was still more so in personal intercourse. Kenneth never controverted anything, never wanted reasons for anything;—that faith in God's personal fatherly love, that good news of redemption, which was Kate's joy, seemed to have neither repulsion nor attraction for her brother. He admired it very much as a phase of Christianity particularly suited to make perfect women,—and so he was content to leave it. Yet his whole nature seemed more earnest; some deep feeling seemed to have possessed him and deepened every other feeling. Any one who reads this history will doubtless know what it was, but, except Kenneth, no one whom this history mentions, viewing it each from his own particular standing-point, had any suspicion. Kenneth had not known it long. How the love which had been so patronizing, familiar, and unconscious,—had gradually grown reverent and conscious,—and had come to throw him farther and farther from its object, instead of bringing him nearer,—as the child he had petted and teased had grown into the woman he loved,—and the play-fellow had become the holy presence in the inmost sanctuary of his heart,—he perceived not himself until she had been enshrined there long. Did Annie perceive it too?

He scarcely dared ask himself,—how then venture to risk the destruction of all, the reality of old affection and the beautiful dream of this new love, at once, by asking her? A thousand times he had made up his mind to risk all the next time they were alone; but they were so often alone; their intimacy, her confidence, seemed to form the most insuperable barrier; and so, after a minute or two's silence, he generally entered into an energetic conversation on anything, from ecclesiastical architecture to the weather, to prevent her suspecting what he nevertheless longed for her to know.

Once they were in the garden alone on an autumnal evening, and he had flowers in his hand ready to offer her, with all his heart and soul besides; but Annie took them so naturally that he could not say a word beside some grave commonplaces on botany, which Annie seemed to think very appropriate, and just what he meant to say.

Once he met her returning from some

charitable expedition, and walked home with her in a thunderstorm; and between the danger and the umbrella there seemed no escape. But Annie clung so confidingly to his arm, not relinquishing it when she found the shelter of a shed in the fields, that it would have seemed absolute treachery to do anything but wonder when the rain would stop.

Once they were reading together a love-scene in one of Schiller's plays, but Annie read on so simply, that all Kenneth's efforts were directed to prevent her noticing the tremulous emotion of his voice.

So the time fixed for Kenneth to go on the Continent came and passed, and a new date was fixed, and new excuses framed, until at length Mr. Cameron peremptorily insisted on the passage being taken in the steamer.

Mrs. Cameron had packed the portmanteau, —and his *compagnon de voyage* had arrived, —and the last evening had come. The last evening came, the two families met, Kenneth and Annie played chess, and rambled in the garden,—and Kate and Kenneth's friend disagreed, laughed, discussed, and were friends,—and Mrs. Fielding gave parting warnings about the seductions of Romanism, —and Mrs. Cameron remembered two or three additional comforts for the voyage down the Nile, which every one had to help to get ready in time,—and the evening was over, and Annie was gone with nothing beyond a brotherly parting, half in laughter, half in tears.

It would certainly be easier to write. He would write to her from off Gibraltar, or from the Pyramids, or Jerusalem, or anywhere a thousand miles off; distance would remove the barrier between them, and bring them near again. And yet a word from her, what a holy charm and weight of hope to bear with him, and keep his heart firm and fixed in all the vicissitudes and excitements of that journey. He would see her yet. But they were to leave at ten the next morning; how could it be managed? The difficulty increased his feeling of the necessity. Annie, he knew, rose early, and he resolved to see her the next morning before breakfast.

When he awoke on the morrow, he wondered at his own audacity—it seemed madness—but seven o'clock struck, at nine they were to breakfast, and in three hours they would be underweigh for Egypt—not a moment for reconsidering anything. Before eight, Kenneth was at the Rectory. Annie was in the garden. He had invited her to walk with him to Eastwood to breakfast, but it seemed like subterfuge, and he simply led her through the open window into that little room which was more especially her own.

The flowers he had given her on that evening, when they were alone, were on the piano. He saw that, and the books he had given her, in an instant. Where feeling does not blind, it gives a strange mesmeric acuteness to every sense. And then he confessed how he loved her. She made no answer, but turned pale and cold almost as death. Then clearly and without hesitation he told her the history of his love, how it had grown and changed with her, and now possessed him altogether, not with the impetuous force of a new passion, but the strength and tenderness of an affection which had grown with and around the roots of his heart, and was as imperishable and as much part of himself as his love even for Kate, and as sacred as his reverence for God. She looked down for some moments and said nothing, her face flushed crimson and white by turns, and at length settled into a calm paleness.

"You do not love me, Annie, you cannot understand me—do not fear to say so. I am leaving England to-day—forget these moments—think I was mad—perhaps I am."

He said these words with an almost harsh rapidity of tone and utterance, and still she sat motionless and silent. He added in a low, trembling voice, "Only say so, Annie."

She raised her eyes to his for a moment,

but in that moment their souls met. He felt that she loved him. And was not that enough? Was not that all?

What though her face remained as still and pale as before, and she turned it from him, and the hand he had taken, as he seated himself near her, lay cold and passive in his? she did not withdraw it, and did not that express enough?

She did not withdraw her hand, but turning her pale face towards him, and looking up at him with an expression of deep and sorrowful earnestness, she said at length, calmly, but almost in a whisper,

"Kenneth, it cannot be; our faith is not the same."

"You shall teach me, Annie. I will follow you, learn from you, and grow like you."

"I should love you too much, Kenneth. I dare not."

He pleaded and argued, at first half-playfully; her objection seemed to him such a feather in the current of their common love

—would she sacrifice him to a creed? Then, as he became convinced of her earnestness, that it was another feeling stronger even than her love to him, not a mere opinion which opposed him, his entreaties became more incoherent and passionate; would she cut him off from the only influence that ever could lead him to good? would she place that awful barrier between him and the change she desired to see in him, of making every holy impulse and impression suspected by himself, by the question, did it spring from the sense of God's love, or the longing for hers?

Still, although Annie's lip quivered, and her voice became almost inaudible, her answer did not change.

"You would reign in my heart, and not God. It would separate us, Kenneth, not unite us. I can ask God to bless you now, as I could not then, for I know I should be disobeying Him."

Then, in his sorrow, he said many bitter

things;—she thought him a heathen,—she would cast off and abandon the sinner—was that like Christ?

The tears came in her eyes, although they did not flow, and choked her voice as she murmured, "O, Kenneth!"

That tone changed the whole current of his feeling at once, and again he began to plead, until, as he saw how it distressed although it could not move her, he suddenly checked himself, and with one strong effort, in a tone in which pride and tenderness, and resentment and reverence, strangely met, he said,

"Forgive me, Annie. God bless you."

And in another minute he was beyond the garden, and on his way to Eastwood.

Left in the room alone, for the first time Annie's resolution failed,—had she done right? Had she indeed been like the Pharisee rather than the Saviour? She would have recalled Kenneth, but it was too late. She could not shed a tear. She could not collect her thoughts. Kenneth's arguments came whirling and eddying through her heart, until her own seemed mere flimsy words before them. The voice, which had seemed heavenly, was carried away like a weak breeze in the sudden rush of the torrent, and borne with it. She could not consult any one; it seemed as if the only Counselor she could have fled to abandoned her in the storm, and so, mechanically and like an automaton, she passed through the duties of the day.

At last the evening came, and she had a right, without neglecting any one, to be once more alone. She sat down on the low Derby chair her little brothers and sisters had given her on her last birthday, by the little table on which lay her Bible and one or two old favorite books, beside the little white tent-bed. The familiar objects which at first grated like a monotonous discord on her new grief, her new unsuspected love, and her new strange sorrow, gradually breathed over her, with all their associations, a feeling of quiet, and recalled her to her natural course of thought and affection. She took up her Bible, at first mechanically, but verse after verse spoke to her with a voice that gathered strength and distinctness as she read on, until she paused at the words,

"The Father himself loveth you."

She felt Him there with her, watching her; her Father in heaven—and she had known Him long.

She leant her spirit on Him, as she would have leant her aching head on a mother's breast, and wept abundantly—feeling His love and resting on it.

She thought, "If I could only do anything, sacrifice anything, for Kenneth!"—and she wept and sobbed as if her heart would break; but she wept as a child, a child of God, without bitterness or rebellion, and those tears relieved her heart. Then remembering dimly a passage in an old quaint book which lay by chance on her table, she turned to it and read, "A man may love another as his own soul, yet, perhaps, that love of his cannot help him; he may thereby pity him in prison, but not relieve him; bemoan him in misery, but not help him; suffer with him in trouble, but not ease him. We cannot love grace into a child, nor mercy into a friend; we cannot love them into heaven, though it may be the great desire of our soul. But now the love of Christ, being the love of God, is effectual in producing all the good things that He willeth unto His beloved—love, grace, and holiness." And, believing in that wonderful and mighty love of His, she prayed to Him long and fervently for Kenneth and herself, and afterwards laid down to rest, and slept.

XVII.

PERPLEXITIES, READY-MADE AND HOME-MADE.

We never know a sorrow until it has been a night with us. It is the first waking which stamps it on us as no dream, but a companion from whom we cannot fly, a burden we must bear with us in all our duties and projects, and cannot lay down for an instant. Heavily did the new trial weigh on Annie when she woke; but she had long ceased to meet any trial or perplexity alone, and before her heart was wearied with buffeting with its strength, or her mind bewildered with measuring its long results of possible sorrow, she laid it all once more before her God, and sought strength and direction, and she found them. It bound her very close to the only Friend in whom she could confide; and often she thought this must be the reason of the chastening, and was able unfeignedly, although with tears, to mingle thanksgiving with her prayer. She could not speak of it to any beside; it was Kenneth's secret as well as hers, and therefore doubly sacred. Besides, who could advise her? Mrs. Fielding would, probably, not only think her right to make the sacrifice, but wrong to deem it a sacrifice. Kate might not agree with her, and she would not for the world lay any part of her grief on her aunt Cameron. There was only Grannie, but she could not lay open her heart even to her; besides, what relief could it bring? The sorrow was there, a real and inevitable weight to be borne—and how could words help it?

Occasionally, when her prayers had been very earnest, a hope flashed across her heart,—but a hope that brought so much tumult with it, that it was more overwhelming than all her fears. She endeavored, therefore, to relinquish it, and sometimes thought she had quite succeeded, and would never associate her own and Kenneth's future life again except as a joy beyond and above this earth altogether; when some trifle would scatter all her heroic resolutions like summer gossamer, and show her what a reserve of timid hopes and sweet dreams had been slumbering beneath; until at length she gave up all her stoic armor, and contented herself with gathering as she needed a stone from the brook cf which she drank by the way, meeting every fresh temptation with fresh prayer, casting herself entirely upon God with all that future into which her restless thoughts peered vainly, like homeless children on a fireside through windows dimmed by their eager breath. She learned to live (as all must learn who would live in peace) from day to day, leaving to-morrow with Him with whom she left the eternity to which "to-morrow" *belongs*. And so through all the tossings of the storm she was advancing, and in all her sinkings of heart she was learning the reality of the support of that Arm beyond which she could not sink.

Then Annie had that best medicine for grief like hers, the perpetual recurrence of duties which could not be neglected, perpetual claims on the sympathy which she had accustomed all around her to trust, duties which, though at first they seem bitter and unpalatable, are soon found to have strengthened the spirit like food.

Kate at the time needed more sympathy than she could give. To the first glow of love to all those who she believed loved her Saviour, succeeded a very great disappointment at the coldness of some, the narrowness of others, and the continued and contented imperfections of almost all.

Grannie was spending the afternoon at Eastwood, and was busily employed and apparently absorbed with four restless needles in certain complicated woolen manufactures. Kate had been writing a note, and was pausing in the labors of composition to make

20

sundry mathematical and other diagrams on the portfolio. At length she said in a dreamy tone,

"I wish I had lived in one of the mornings of history."

"Have you known no day-spring from on high, Kate?" said Grannie, looking up half reproachfully as the needles went rapidly on.

"Indeed, Grannie, I have, and it has guided my feet into the way of peace,—but I was not thinking of myself, but of the world, the Church. Everything seems so old and decrepid now, at least everything human. We seem living just as many good impulses are dying out,—it must be very pleasant to be present when the movement commences."

"Are you thinking of the Reformation?"

"No, I am not so ambitious. When the present evangelical party first arose, and were wondered at, and laughed at, and Missionary Societies were beginning, and every one who was not decidedly asleep was decidedly awake—I should like to have lived then,—before religious societies had become machines, and religious conversation either controversy or gossip; before there was such a thing as the 'religious world.'"

"My dear child, you must go back a long way, before the Epistles, when Diotrephes loved the pre-eminence, and some preached Christ of envy and strife; before the Acts, when the Grecians murmured against the Hebrews, because their widows were neglected; before the Sermon on the Mount, when the vain attempt called forth the warning voice, 'Ye cannot serve God and mammon.'"—

"Before the Fall,—I suppose you will conclude, Grannie."

"At least before the Flood, or the days when Lot lingered in Sodom."

"Still is it not true that some times have more vigor in them than others,—more of the power of Divine life? Religion seems such a cold and smooth thing now—one does not hear of any one being offended or won by it. Think of Whitefield and Zinzendorf. I wonder if it is morning anywhere in the Church just now. To me it seems to be all mid-day or bed-time, petty conflict and traffic, with din and dust, or else a quiet and orderly sleepiness, only fretful if disturbed."

"And are you superior to all these infirmities and evil influences, Kate?" said Grannie, rather severely.

"By no means, Grannie, I suffer from all by turns; it is because I suffer from them and fear them that I long to escape. I am half disposed to be an Irvingite, and believe nothing will ever be right, unless we can get real spiritual apostles and successors of apostles again."

"We need and wait for One mightier than apostles, Kate. But what has made you so discontented? I cannot bear to hear Christians murmuring superciliously at the times they live in, as if the infection of the times were not also in us, and God had not fixed our lot in time as well as place. There is, I think, only one safe way of preventing such complaints from becoming murmurs, and that is by turning them into confessions."

"Well, dear Grannie," said Kate, laying aside her excursive pen and cheerfully taking up some crochet work, "I believe I was put thoroughly out of humor with myself and everybody else at aunt Fielding's party last night. There were so many really Christian people there, and I expected to be so cheered and refreshed; but we had music and compliments, and a great deal of politics and agriculture, and a little missionary intelligence, and then like a snowball fell amongst us the announcement of family prayer. After that the tone of the conversation in some measure changed, but the nearest approach to religious intercourse I heard were lamentations over the absurdities of Romanists and the irregularities of Dissenters; on which, I am sorry to say, the spirit of perversity got possession of me, and I began to talk to my little cousin Elinor about the piety of Fénélon, and the labors of the London Missionaries in the Pacific, and thereupon was involved in a warm discussion with aunt Fielding. So I came away unrefreshed and penitent, leaving aunt Fielding in doubt whether to class me with the Jesuits or the Plymouth Brethren, doing harm and getting no good. And yet this was an unexceptionable party. No one would of dreamt of cards or dancing, and our hearts were all probably set on one object. Why cannot the intercourse of Christians be Christian?"

"You are not thirty yet, Kate, and so perhaps hardly old enough for an ecclesiastical reformer. Christians do, in some places, meet to read the Bible, and pray and sing hymns together; as you cannot introduce that here, or mould other people's hearts, would it not be wiser to keep your own fresh and full? You can read with Annie, you know."

"But are there not peculiar difficulties in

the way of a simple Christian course in these days, Grannie? The Church is so luxurious and so like the world."

"'The world' is no new enemy, Kate, as the Catechism might have taught you; and it is a subtle enemy. If it were to come to you and say, 'I am the world, one of your three sworn foes, give me a lodging in your heart,' you would probably not listen, and therefore it says no such thing, but rather, 'I am influence, I am common sense, I am prudence, I am refinement, I am intellect—surely you will not exclude such a valuable friend?' And few do in all forms—none except those who remember that the whole of life is a pilgrimage and a warfare. Rampart within rampart it follows you, and although it would indeed be folly to sally forth and encounter it on its own ground, you need more strength than your own to overcome it even in the sphere of duty."

"But seriously and humbly, Grannie, speaking of it as a disease which I dread because liable to the infection, is there not a real and lamentable dryness and narrowness about many of those we really feel and know to be living by that new and eternal life which was with the Father, and was manifested unto us—a phraseology by which the largest and deepest truths slip over the heart as smoothly and ineffectually as a snow-ball; as if the pure waters had been frozen and polished for the convenience of transportation. I feel sometimes, Grannie, as if nothing would do some I know so much good as a good course of astronomy, enabling them to feel God, not as word in a text, or a party in a theological or ecclesiastical contest, but as the Maker of not only countless worlds, but countless systems of worlds. Then, from that to come back to the Bible, and feel Him near to us as the Father, becoming man to redeem us—Grannie, it seems as if some never thought for an instant what the incarnation was."

"Pray and seek, my child, to have such

lowly and overpowering, and yet personal and steadfast thoughts of Him, and you may be a little well of water springing up in the wilderness yourself. Each of us might be. I cannot deny the truth of much that you say. I fear evangelical faith has, with many, become a mere human and traditional thing, and with most, in some measure so; and as such it has no more life than any other human religion. For the life is not in the creed, but in Him in whom we believe. Now, are you ready to go and see old Honor Burden?—she is worse—and told me she enjoyed your last visit and reading to her."

Kate would have lingered to prolong the conversation, but she overcame the inertia, and went away repeating to herself,

> Denn alles muss in Nichts zerfallen
> Wenn es im Seyn beharren will.

And when she had sat some time by the bedside in the low dark room, and read some verses of the Bible, and seen the reality of its messages in the calm firmness of the heart which rested on them on the very edge of the unfathomed grave, and came back to her own sweet home, she felt that spiritually as well as bodily she was in the fresh open air again.

XVIII.

PERPLEXITIES, READY-MADE AND HOME-MADE.

"Do you remember, Annie," said Kate, as they left Grannie one morning, "some months ago, as we passed just here, my saying, I would not wish for a higher ideal than Grannie's life, to be a nun without vows?"

"I do," said Annie, rejoicing at the moment in her close cottage bonnet.

"You did not agree with me, you know."

"I did not," rejoined Annie with a quivering voice, wondering what Kate would say or ask next.

"You had truer ideas than I of home, then,—still I should like to find some community of people, one day, who were really living entirely and heartily to obey and serve Christ."

Annie, greatly relieved at the turn in the conversation, repeated those beautiful lines from the most perfect of practical hymns,

> "Most careful not to *serve* thee much,
> But *please* thee perfectly."

Kate, whose trains of thought, when once the steam was up, were not easily checked, continued,

"What do you think, Annie, one day of your and my becoming Moravian sisters?"

"I am afraid you would find a considerable deficiency of those courses of astronomy and geology you have been talking of lately, dear Kate."

"Ah, but that would be no deficiency there. They arrive at the same results another way. Their minds, doubtless, expand by the force of their hearts. They see the universe in God, and become wiser than the teachers, by the strength of loving and serving. They *live* really, Annie, and suffer and sacrifice really. I think, whatever you may intend for yourself, I shall join a Moravian sisterhood one day,—not now, you understand, but by and by."

"Dear Kate, how can you plan anything beyond your home?"

"O yes, but every one has not always a home. Do you never dream beyond to-day, Annie?"—Annie did not answer.—"And if you have your sweet visions of 'parsonages and pony-carriages,' why may I not have mine of Hospitals and Hottentot Missionary Stations?" And she went on half earnestly and half playfully, whilst Annie endeavored to listen with interest.

Half an qour afterwards Grannie softly entered their little room, and saw, as she sat with her back to the light, the tears falling fast on the little socks she was knitting for her youngest brother. Grannie watched her in silence for a moment, then gently laid her hand on her shoulder, and said,

"My poor Annie, what has happened?"

Annie looked up and endeavored to meet Grannie's eye with her own cheerful smile, but the effort was too much, and instead she burst into a flood of irrepressible tears. "It seems so strange that Kate should make sorrows for herself, Grannie."

"We often do," said Grannie gently, "until God makes them for us. Have you anything on your conscience, Annie?"

Annie looked up with a bright frank smile through her tears, and said, "That is my great comfort." And drop by drop her heart poured out its griefs and anxieties.

Grannie did not attempt soothing or comfort. She pressed Annie's head on her breast, and said with a trembling voice,

"My God, I thank thee for this victory."

"Oh Grannie, it is no victory—I have not overcome—I am só weak and sinful, and so ungrateful."

"The best victories are those won through weakness, Annie. My child, my precious child, to *you it is given* not only to believe but also to suffer for His sake."

"But for *him*, Grannie, how can I do anything for him?"

"You have done the utmost you could do for him. You have shown him the reality of those things in which you believe."

"Ah, I fear not.—He thinks me bigoted, unjust, a Pharisee, cold-hearted," and her voice was choked with tears.

"I am sure, in his inmost heart, he does not, dearest child. Trust, Annie, trust. God has given you strength, and He has abundant blessing in store for you."

"Oh Grannie, do you think so?" she murmured, clinging to these words as to a prophecy.

"I am no prophetess, Annie—I have no new promises to make you, I can only point you to the old promises, which have never failed, but," she added in a low voice, "I can tell you an old history which may encourage you,"—and after a minute's pause she continued abruptly, "I was once engaged, Annie, to an officer in the navy. He was at sea when an entire change came over all my thoughts and feelings—gradually but clearly God revealed Himself to me, and fixed my affections on things above. He had no knowledge or care for religion beyond a vague reverence. I wrote to him candidly all I felt. He wrote back saying, he should only love me more; all that I had said was beautiful; he had often himself felt God's voice in the storm, and he believed it was impossible for a sailor to be an atheist; of course men could not be as gentle and angelic as women, but he was sure he should never disturb or oppose anything I thought right. This did not satisfy me, and I wrote again, endeavoring to show him that the blessed message I had received was a message for all, and that it was necessary to our future happiness that we should not only bear with one another, but be of one heart in these things; that without this, indeed, we could never be happy. The next mail was late—I thought it would never come. At length, one evening when we had a dinner-party at the house, it came. A few short cold lines, saying that I need seek no further excuse for withdrawing from an engagement which was no longer a source of happiness to me, he would on no account fetter me—from henceforth he should consider me free, and would pray that I might find elsewhere the union of heart I no longer felt with him. Every word of that letter branded itself into my brain. I had braced myself to no such purpose; I had never contemplated such a sacrifice, or if the possibility crossed me, I had banished it, and sought to bury its memory in a thousand arguments. Yet when this letter came I dared not write to contradict it. My pride resented it, although that would soon have melted, but conscience could not fly from the truth thus forced upon her. That evening I was more gay and self-possessed than was common with me; the timidity which usually made me constrained and silent had vanished. My father kissed me fondly when the company had left, and said he must send a glowing account of me to Maurice; those words broke down all my pride and strength, and placing the letter in his hands, I rushed from the room. But I will not weary you with these details,—every event of those few days comes out as vividly and minutely from the rest of my life as a piece of miniature painting in a rough sketch —they were burnt in, and I only wish to recall what may comfort you, my child. My father thought the letter a mere subterfuge. I knew it was not that, but he would not believe me, Annie, and in spite of all my entreaties wrote a reply even more concise and cutting. The next I heard of Maurice, Annie, was that he was the gayest and wildest man at Malta, and after that, that he had married a lovely and amiable girl, quite a love-match, they said,—I trust it was, although I could hardly bring myself to wish it then. And so he misunderstood me to the end. I never heard from him again. But ten years ago, Annie, he died, died they said with these words on his lips, 'God loves you, Jesus loves you, He has opened heaven for you,'—they were from my last letter."

Annie wept more than before. Grannie did not weep, but she said, "Was not that enough, Annie? I feel I could not have done without one stroke of that long sorrow; God had another course of life for me, and it has not been lonely nor sad."

Annie pressed Grannie's hand thankfully, but she could not help trembling with the fear that such a life might be appointed her, and she said at length,

"But, Grannie, all that would be very sad to look forward to—I am afraid I cannot wish it."

"My dear child," said Grannie, smiling, "do not on any account look forward to anything of the kind. I only want you to look forward to the answer to my prayers as the end. That was so bright, that I forgot how long and dark the waiting might seem to you.

Do not look forward, looking forward only strains the eyes—looking upward brings down the blessing."

"Have I been wrong, Grannie," said Annie at last, when they had had a walk to freshen her tearful face and were nearly at home again; "have I been wrong to seek sympathy and comfort from you, when God Himself had been so gracious to me, and had indeed comforted me?"

"What an idea are you forming of God, Annie? Who gave me to you? Who planted sympathy in my heart, and gave me sorrow that I might learn how to comfort you? Besides, my child, do you think you give me nothing back for what I give you? I need you, Annie, if you are too independent to need me, and I cannot do without you and your confidence. You have strengthened my heart to-day, Annie. You are the first to whom I ever told all this."

And from that day Annie's sorrow, though it weighed on her still as a heavy burden, was less like a dark secret spell; it seemed no longer such a singular and awful thing; others had suffered likewise,—and Grannie prayed with her, and hoped with her, until the hope became a substantial thing to both, although Annie could not help secretly hoping it would not end quite the same for her as for Grannie.

XIX.

A NEW ELEMENT.

"I WILL tell you an allegory, Annie," said Kate.

They were on the rock in Robinson Crusoe's island, which had been their granary in days of yore. Annie was standing with folded hands taking mental daguerreotypes of the things around, above, and beneath,—clear full clouds setting in silver patches of the bluest sky; flowers, mint, ragwort, and wild geranium, and wet leaves, glistening and trembling with the fresh rain-drops,—the river exulting in its new wealth of waters,—all things testifying to the late intermingling of earth and heaven. Kate had been sketching, and continued throwing in points of light and shade as she spoke. "If you will be good and not interrupt, Annie, I will tell you a story. Once upon a time a fisherman's family were sent by their father, who was engaged on a distant point of the coast, to the sea-shore to save as many as possible from the crew of a ship which had just been wrecked. They were provided with life-boats and restoratives from the Humane Society. There were ten children. When the father came to see with what diligence they labored, and what success they had met, he found one applying the remedies to a pale and apparently lifeless body, resting the pale head on her bosom, and chafing the cold limbs—two administering food and cordials to a group of rescued ones—and two more still buffeting the waves that dashed against the shattered vessel, and picking up here one and there another who were clinging to staves and broken pieces of the ship. He could see nothing of the rest until he turned a rock which hid the ship from view. There he discovered the remaining five; they also were busy, and seemed fully impressed with the importance of their avocations. One was making an artistic representation of a shipwreck on the sand, and endeavoring with the same sand to keep off the waves which were effacing it—another was laboriously analyzing the medicines of the Humane Society—a third was weeping over the loss of the Royal George—a fourth was especially and most importantly busy constructing the model of a life-boat on mathematical principles, the old ones being, he said, unscientific—and the fifth was asleep. They were all eager to prove to the father their diligence and ability. 'But what,' he asked, 'is becoming of the wreck meanwhile?' At that moment a piercing death-shriek answered his question, and the sleeper started up and rubbing his eyes, exclaimed, 'Was I dreaming? I thought I had just rescued half the crew!'—Annie, Annie," she continued after a minute, laying down her drawing, "on which side of the rock are we? Or rather," she added, "am

I? How little I *fear* for others, how little I *love*, how little I *do!*"

"Dearest Kate," said Annie, "I am sure I feel the same. Yet I think we must be not impatient, or imagine every one has to do the same work. There are other things, you know, to be done even for shipwrecked people beyond and after saving them from being drowned. Our work, as the women of the family, may, in general, lie more inland."

Kate smiled. "You are right. I will not give up drawing and music, or anything, until something better demands the time. If we are only called to boil the kettle for the shipwrecked sailors, or air the linen for them by the cottage fire-side, we must not let the linen burn, or the kettle boil over. Will that do, Annie? have I learned my lesson?"

"I mean," said Annie, "that I think we are called to be servants and soldiers, and not knights-errant."

"My dear little wise Annie, I am content! only I hope it is not ambitious to trust I may not be set to boil the kettle all my life." And, gathering up the sketching materials, the cousins hurried up the old kitchen garden before the next shower came.

"Do you know, Annie," said Kate, as they rested under the shelter of the recess of the wall, "we are all very much disappointed in Kenneth?"

Annie was silent.

"He will not enter into papa's business. He says he could not bear to live at Milbourne all his life."

Annie murmured something which Kate took for a reply, or a sign of attention.

"It is certainly very ungrateful and uncivil to us all, but he talks of taking pupils at Oxford and distinguishing himself as a literary man. You know he took honors. Things have not been looking very bright lately, and Kenneth is a dear generous fellow; he will not ask a shilling of allowance, and says papa wants some one more experienced, and with some capital, to take part of the burden of anxiety off him. And so papa has taken a partner."

"Who is he?" asked Annie, with an eagerness which made Kate look at her in amazed curiosity.

"A Mr. Miller, some good practical man of business, I believe," replied Kate carelessly; "but is not Kenneth a dear noble willful fellow?"

"He always was generous," said Annie.

"Why, you are crying, Annie! Well, I very nearly did at first. I am so sorry Kenneth is not to be with us, and so glad he has done as he has. O Annie, he must be brought right at last."—Annie made no answer.—"We do not often speak of him, but I cannot tell you how often he is in my thoughts, Annie. Do you pray for him?"

"Yes," was the low reply.

"Yes, yes," continued Kate, "I know you do, dear loving Annie. I need not have asked." Annie felt as if she were a traitor to every one she loved.

But Kate continued giving stories and incidents from Kenneth's travels.—"He writes in such excellent spirits," she said. "I never knew him say so little about wishing to see us all again. But he never writes an earnest or religious sentence. He seems to be living objectively altogether, in and for the beautiful, wonderful, changing world around him." Annie drank in every word, but only questioned by her attentive silence.

And so the shower passed, and they reached the house. When they entered the drawing-room, a gentleman was waiting there alone. Kate never remembered seeing him, but she concluded at once it was the new partner—a person whom, from some undefined idea that he was a usurper of Kenneth's place in the world, she was by no means disposed to like. He was leaning on the mantel-piece, apparently gazing into the mirror, the worst place any man could be caught standing in, Kate concluded, and was withdrawing accordingly, with a demure courtesy, when the stranger advanced easily towards her, and said:

"Miss Cameron, may I introduce myself? I think I had the pleasure of seeing you ten years since."

"Decidedly cool," Kate thought, but she recalled Annie, and seated herself. The stranger wore spectacles, so that his age and expression were indeterminable; and although Kate was disposed to resent his memory, there was something so unfeignedly respectful about his manner, easy and unembarrassed as it was, that in a few moments she forgot it altogether, and was engaged in recalling the occasion of that first meeting, and explaining, as the circumstances were gradually brought back, the cause of Annie's and her own irruption into the counting-house at the memorable era of Robinson Crusoe's island. So that when Mr. Cameron appeared no further introduction was needed.

Kate was, however, not quite pleased with herself for so soon losing sight of her resentment at Mr. Miller's usurpation; and at dinner she was unusually silent and critical. Once, at dessert, she heard Mr. Miller say to her mother, "The Bible, and the Bible alone, is the religion of Protestants." A common-place which so offended her, although the tone was very earnest, that some of her old traditional prejudices were restored for a minute to a galvanic vivacity, and she said to Annie in a low voice as they left the dining-room, "To think of any one venturing that quotation out of Exeter Hall."

"I rather like Mr. Miller," said Mrs. Cameron, as she established herself on the sofa, "don't you, Kate?"

"I hardly think I do, mamma," replied Kate, and to avoid discussion she struck some chords on the piano.

Whether it was on account of the music or the lack of subjects in the dining-room, the gentlemen soon re-appeared. Kate continued playing dreamily some airs of Mendelssohn. Mr. Miller did not approach the piano until she concluded, and then he drew near and asked if she played anything of Mozart's. Kate played some airs and variations rather carelessly.

"Mozart is such a tune-maker," she said, being in a paradoxical humor, "he seems always to be making ribbon-patterns out of nature, as they say those who live by such designs do, cutting clouds, and flowers, and fields into pretty colored strips, with one idea perpetually repeated."

Mr. Miller smiled, but did not take up her image; he said simply, "My mother is so fond of Mozart,—I feel more at home with Bethooven. Bethooven always reminds me of Luther,—no finery, no trifling, but all so grand and earnest; even the scherzos are earnest, like children at play."

Kate concluded he was a musical amateur, and she hated musical amateurs, at least Englishmen who pretended to be so, and she replied,

"I suppose we are not born to an inheritance of music in England; the merest school-boy in Germany knows more and can sing better than our connoisseurs."

"Hardly that, I think, although most of the children in Prussia do learn to sing in parts at the eight years' schools, and in Bohemia they are born to sing as naturally as to speak. I was reading somewhere the other day, that in Queen Elizabeth's time music was as universal a taste and pleasure in England as it is now in Germany."

"Yes," rejoined Kate, "the Puritans were not all Luthers, or it might have been otherwise."

"No, indeed; but what rejoiced me in this same book," he replied, "was, that the destruction of a national musical taste, at least as regards religious music, was traced to the affectations of the Restoration rather than to the austerities of the Commonwealth."

"Yet neither the Hussites, nor the Thirty Years' War seem, from your account, to have destroyed the taste in Bohemia."

"I speak of national songs and melodies there, but I know personally little of Bohemia. The Moravian Brethren certainly have a sweet and noble church music."

"You know something of them?" Kate asked.

"My mother is a descendant of the old Brethren's Church," he replied, "and my father was a Lutheran."

"Where does Mr. Miller come from, papa?" she asked the next morning at breakfast.

"I believe he is of German origin, although he has lived chiefly in England—he spells his name in a queer way, with a *u* and two dots—you know best how that should be pronounced, Kate. The family have handed down hereditarily some of the old Bohemian secrets of coloring glass, which I hope we shall find of some use."

XX.

DISCORDS RESOLVED.

Mr. Müller was necessarily much at the house, and more than necessarily much in the garden and on the moors with Mrs. Cameron, Kate, and Annie.

Kate's objection to his intrusion seemed gradually weakening, although she still asserted that he was the most uninteresting person in the world to argue with, because he was always so in earnest he would not let one enjoy a paradox, and could not behave to an error, however ingenious or brilliant, with any amount of politeness.

He seldom obtruded religious conversation, and yet, when he was present, the conversation seemed naturally to take a higher tone, and the current to set heavenwards, as if every one felt there was one who could always respond most warmly to whatever was best. In those party questions which commonly pass for religious conversation, he never joined. Kate could not quite understand whether because he objected to them, or because he differed from every one. The few words he spoke on such controversies seemed to her, however, peculiarly clear, as if he saw such questions *from above*, and formed materials for many subsequent reflections.

He had the faculty of making every one earnest, and getting at their real thoughts and feelings—not from any remarkable penetration, but from the mere infection of his sincerity.

Nothing could be more frank and natural than his manner,—and yet Kate never felt so much with any one as if there were a world behind to which she could not penetrate. He never said brilliant and pointed things,—and yet Kate never thought any words so striking, or any gaiety so infectious. With him she felt in some sense a happy child again. From the first week of their acquaintance they seemed naturally to belong to one another; and what one said always had some unconscious reference to the other. He often spoke to her of his mother and one sister, and they had become to her what the people in her story-books had been when she was a child, beings to dream about and picture, and hold imaginary conversations with. A deep and holy union of heart was forming between them; but so quietly and gently, that it needed some sudden shock to startle it into consciousness.

One morning they were rambling in some meadows near a railway, which had recently whirled Milbourne into connection with the great world beyond.

They had been talking about railways, and electric telegraphs, and universal peace, and the brotherhood of men, and the commercial millennium,—and watching a group of children who were playing on the other side of the embankment. There were four, and a little toddling creature who had been set down for a moment to amuse himself with a daisy chain. They stood and watched the group, when suddenly the baby seeing Kate and a little dog that was gamboling about her, stretched out his little hands to her, and was beginning to creep across to her. At that instant the whistle was heard. Kate screamed to the child and motioned him away with her hands, moving towards him. Mr. Müller, gently pushing her away, darted across the line. She saw his foot slip just as he reached the child, and then the whole train rushed past and hid them both. That indivisible point of time was by her heart divided into an age of vivid agony, fear, and prayer,—and then she scarcely saw, but felt with every sense that he stood opposite her safe with the child in his arms. In another instant he was at her side and the baby in her arms, wondering at the tears which in Kate's despite fell silently on his face, and making unequivocal demonstrations that he did not mistake her for any of his relations. The mother fortunately soon appeared, and with a torrent of gratitude to Mr. Müller, and love to the baby, and indignation against the children, left Kate and Mr. Müller to pursue their way home. Neither of them said much, but Kate did not refuse to rest her hand on his arm.

The next day Mr. Müller went to pay a visit to his family, and the next came a letter for Kate—and on the next Kate had ceased to consider the Moravian sister-house the ideal of a future home.

It was certainly an unsatisfactory engagement for people to discuss—so convenient and smooth, exactly what it ought to have been, that there was absolutely nothing to be said about it.

Mrs. Fielding wondered who would ever have dreamt of Kate's doing anything so sensible; and Grannie, who saw all these things in rather a romantic way, with the eyes of her own early and unfaded love, was most tender and full in her sympathy. The only one whose approbation, and affection and love for her friend, Kate half-doubted, was Kenneth. Gerard Müller was so simple in his faith, and so uncompromising and straightforward in his statements of it, that she feared Kenneth might shrink from him. But at length Kenneth came, and Kate's fears were speedily banished. He seemed to like Gerard at once, and told Kate one or two new proofs of his generosity and integrity with regard to the business—and said, he thought them the happiest people he had seen since he left England. He was especially pleased also with Gerard's mother—she seemed all motherliness, he said—and her simple heartedness was the most refreshing thing he had felt for years. Kate was charmed with her brother, and thought him handsomer, and dearer, and more amusing than ever. At least she thought so on the first evening of his return. The next morning she traced a look of lassitude and pain, and she feared ill-health under his bronzed complexion, which had deceived her by candle-light; and when he had been a few days at Eastwood, she wondered how she could have thought his letters buoyant and cheerful. He spoke so much as if all his heart were frozen into seeing and willing, and he had become a mere spectator of all that stirs its deepest feelings. Gradually, in the light of her own happy love, the perception of his dawned upon her. She watched him, and observed Annie's gentle pale face, until the whole sad history revealed itself to her, and bound her at once to Annie and to her brother with a tenfold tenderness.

The only one with whom Kenneth seemed quite unconstrained and at home was Gerard's mother, who had now taken a small house near Milbourne with her son and her only daughter, an illustrated edition of

Hermann's Dorothea. She was a dear, simple old lady, with that soft, half-plaintive voice and quiet emphasis of intonation which some German women peculiarly possess—which seems as if learned in rocking their children's cradles. She had had little extent of education, and seen little of the world. Her books were almost all religious books, and many of these were seldom opened. The only histories she seemed thoroughly acquainted with were those of the Bible, of the Moravian churches and missions, and her own earnest and undramatic life. She was not intellectual, nor enthusiastic, nor remarkable in any way, except it might be for a faith as vivid as a child's in her Saviour, and a quiet love to Him, which seemed to be deeper in her heart even than that to her "blessed" husband and her children, and to unite her to all who loved Him in sincerity with a love as real and calm as that of kindred.

It was amazing what an amount of work

Mrs. Müller accomplished with her calm, slow utterance, and her manner, which it was impossible to discompose. She was very much taken with Jean, and said she reminded her of "a true German house-mother,"—a title which, in the hurry of other events, I had forgotten to mention, had, within the last few months, become Jean's due.

Kate loved her exceedingly, as was natural; but what the fascination she exercised over Kenneth was, she could scarcely comprehend. Mrs. Müller seemed never to be endeavoring to exercise influence over any one, yet her presence and her heart seemed to lull his heart to rest.

Grannie and Mrs. Müller were close friends in a week; and Kate laughingly said she should never forget her look of wonder and disappointment when she discovered that the gentle Annie, on whom her eyes had rested affectionately at their first introduction, was not her son's bride.

Could, O could it be possible that her

child-like faith was winning a way for the truths she believed into Kenneth's heart? Kenneth went away in a few weeks to arrange about pupils at Oxford, but returned after a short absence looking more out of health. Then he would go and sit for hours alone with Mrs. Müller. Dorothea, and Kate, and Gerard, and the rest were making excursions among the beautiful valleys and moorlands around—for it was now acknowledged in the family that Kenneth was in bad health, and long expeditions were forbidden him, and rest peremptorily prescribed. At length a more bracing air was recommended him, and the family, at least Mrs. Cameron and Kate, determined on a visit to the western coast.

But before they left, Kate could not resist asking Mrs. Müller about Kenneth, telling her her own anxieties and entreating her prayers. She began therefore in their last interview,

"Kenneth is a great deal with you,

Madame mère," she said, calling her by the name Kenneth had given her.

"Yes—I am very fond of the dear boy."

"Does he read to you?—or do you talk all the time?"

"He reads to me."

"From what book?" asked Kate, trembling with eagerness.

"From this," said Mrs. Müller quietly, laying her hand on an old copy of Luther's "German Bible for the German nation." "He offered to read it me at first, that I might correct his pronunciation, and give him my Saxon accent, which he thinks sweet."

"Does he ever say anything about what he reads?"

"O yes—we have long chats."

"You must differ very much—but he was always gentle in discussion."

"We never discuss—I am not clever enough for that, dear child."

"But you tell him plainly what you believe, and speak to him plainly," she continued fervently; "you can, he will listen to you."

"Certainly, I say what I think, dear child, and we speak of Him we love—what else should we speak of?"

"O, dear Mrs. Müller, did you say *we* love?"

"Indeed yes, dear child—why do you ask? Your brother's heart seems full of these things. I never saw any one receive the blessed gospel more simply, although he says scarcely anything. He talks sometimes about Zinzendorf and the Greenland missions, as if he longed to labor there, although he never said so."

Kate kissed Mrs. Müller in an ecstacy, and wept and sobbed as if her heart would break, until the calm old lady grew seriously alarmed for her health and sanity.

"My dear child," she murmured, "what can I do for you? What has happened?"

Then Kate became composed, and pressing

Mrs. Müller's hand, she kissed her again, and rose to leave the room. But before she went out of the door she turned and said softly, but emphatically, "Only do not let him think of the Greenland missions."

Mrs. Müller might be reflecting on Kenneth, and fancying she saw in him some of her own single-heartedness, still Kate thought it safe to whisper to Annie as she took leave of her, "Annie, be as much as possible with dear Madame mère whilst I am away." She felt sure they would soon confide in one another.

XXI.

AUTUMN AND ITS HARVEST.

THEY started for the sea-side. They fixed on a quiet group of houses on a lonely part of the coast. Kate formed a thousand plans for winning her way into Kenneth's confidence, and rejected them all when the occasion offered,—or rather the fit occasion never seemed to offer. On the first Sunday after their establishment in the lodgings, as they were returning from the country church, Kenneth himself broke the spell, by saying simply,

"Kate, how much it is to be able to say, 'We thank Thee, O God, for our *creation*.'"

"Yes indeed," Kate replied, "it *is* good to have been born."

"But I never felt that, Kate, I could never

really and solemnly thank God for having created me, until I believed in the inestimable mercy which has redeemed me."

Kate could not reply. She could only hurry home and seek the solitude of her own room.

In the afternoon, as it was too far to attempt a second walk to church, she went out to sit on the rocks with her Bible. Never had its promises seemed more rich and free. It was a lonely place, tall cliffs above and opposite her on the other side of the bay at the head of which she sat; with white waves, in the distance silent and graceful as a

> "Cygne argentée qui s'élève et deploye
> Ses blanches ailes sur les eaux,"

—at her feet curveting, and chasing each other, arching their proud necks, and dashing on the shore, then rolling back over the shingle with a hollow murmur, and falling back from the rocks in cascades and foam of snow—towards the open horizon, gently with sea-green lights and purple shadows; grand ocean-waves, which might have received their first impulse from the shores of the New World. She sat scarcely thinking, or looking, or listening,—in that kind of happy trance when all faculties and senses seem absorbed into one sense of passive enjoyment. Images, thoughts, feelings, floated on her mind, as the sea-mew her eye followed rocked on the wave, as if some other Will were presenting them to her,—and now and then looking down on the Psalms which lay open on her knee,—holy words thrilled through all the beautiful vision, and gathered the scattered tones into chords, to which spiritual human voices seemed to Kate to chant, "We thank thee for our creation."

Kenneth joined her. They entered at once on what filled their hearts.

"I have had many conflicts, Kate," he said; "I did not seek peace,—but it has been given me. I was busy trying to solve all the problems of the universe,—to find out what was wrong there, and set what might be right,—and certainly I found out abundance of wrong, although I advanced very little towards setting it right. I did not acknowledge God. I did not see that He is Himself the only one who can heal and restore—the only Remedy. I was endeavoring to reconcile all the contradictions in the world, Kate, by philosophical theories. You might as well attempt to create an Eden by chemistry or an Adam by machinery. My universe was a poor soulless automaton after all. It was therefore, I think, that all previous efforts to do me good failed. They began with attacking my mechanism, or building up new systems which only encumbered me more, meeting me on my own ground. Mrs. Müller knew nothing of my ground at all, nothing of my difficulties or philosophy, or scientific remedies. But she knew the Lord Jesus Christ and loved Him, and she knew the Bible and believed it. They battered the walls of my ice-fortress, but she sent the sun-beam into its heart. Our sins have cut us off from God, the Fountain of life. 'In Him is life.' He has borne away our sins. The reconciliation is made. The infinite distance is bridged over. I believed in Him—I could not help it. I came to Him; as she spoke of Him I felt Him so near. All that Mrs. Müller said, and read from this book, is so evidently true. She taught me the meaning of the name of Jesus. She led me through Him to the Father, and I found rest."

"And the universe?" Kate said smiling, as she brushed the tears from her cheek.

"It is God's," he replied seriously. "I am but a child in it—yet a living soul—and His child."

Nothing could be happier than that visit. Kate looked back to it often afterwards as a little Arcadia of peace—a place of green pastures and still waters. Gerard came there very often, and they read the Bible together hour after hour, always discovering fresh depths and wonders in it; which was no marvel, when we consider that He who made the heavens, with their golden dust of starry worlds—and the earth with her worlds enfolded in a flower—wrote it.

Kenneth was rather impatient of other religious books. "It is the Old Lamp," he said, "which brings the genii and works the miracles; a lamp to our feet, as we call the sun when we are children, and as we grow up we find it is a world. O Gerard, Kate," he would say, as he lay on the sofa and they read to him, "we are all asleep about the Bible. Christians will surely wake one day and find what a California is at their doors, whilst they are searching heaven and earth for grains of the precious gold."

He grew so rapidly in love and knowledge, they thought he was ripening for years of usefulness on earth. He seemed to think so too. He talked of studying for a missionary life, and they procured him several grammars and dictionaries of various Oriental dialects. "I think I should be best fitted for that station," he said. "I have wandered so far, believed so much error, and there is no way of learning any evil or falsehood so thoroughly as by suffering from it."

Of one subject they had never spoken, until one day when Kate had received a bad account of Annie's health from Mrs. Müller, she said, as they were all sitting together,

"I wish we could have Annie here a little while. I think the sea-air might do her good."

Mrs. Cameron entered into it at once—Gerard was to bring her with him at his next visit, Kate taking care that the invitation should reach Annie as a command from Mrs. Fielding, and not as an entreaty from her. So Annie came. And Kate took especial care to resign her share in Oriental grammar to her on the day after her arrival, and to make Mrs. Cameron preside over her *tete-a-tete* with Gerard in the other room.

When Kate saw Annie next, she was

kneeling by Mrs. Cameron in her bedroom.

"Can you love Annie any better, Kate?" her mother asked. "You must try, for it will be your duty now."

But Annie only met Kate's warm bright greeting with tears.

"You must talk to her, Kate," said Mrs. Cameron, kissing Annie tenderly as she left the room, "she has had more trials than we any of us dreamt of,—and now she cannot believe God is going to make her happy."

"O Kate," Annie said, when they were left alone, "he is so ill."

Kate reasoned, and assured, and half succeeded in inspiring some of her own bright confidence into her cousin.

"He has walked as far as any of us," she said, "until within the last few days,—and he is so energetic and buoyant."

Annie tried to believe it must be so, but when she saw Kenneth, the conviction of the contrary forced itself upon her, and gained terrible strength from day to day.

A few days, however, after this, when the excitement of her arrival had subsided, Kenneth rallied so much that Annie began to think her fears were indeed only the reflex of her love,—the dark spot which dances before the eye after looking at the sun. And she allowed Kenneth to plan in a thousand ways how he would make a missionary life no exile for her, and herself found a thousand schemes for making missionary studies and labors no toil for him.

He took such a healthy interest in the most trifling pleasures and plans,—he could not be so thoroughly an invalid; and Annie insensibly caught his hopefulness, and became assured that a life so pre-occupied with schemes of energetic usefulness, could not soon close. She accepted his projects as prophecies, and to her cheek at least health came back, and firmness to her buoyant tread. The shadow of death, which had passed so near them, only served to deepen their love with the tenderness as of years; whilst the work to which their lives were singly and entirely consecrated, gave to their engagement the solemnity of a sacrament. The were pledged not only for the fire-side, but the battle-field. They were to study, and toil, and endure trial and hardship side by side. There was also a romance about their future, which gave it a peculiar freshness and charm, the lawful romance of true chivalry; prepared as they were with loyal hearts, to shrink from nothing in the service of Him who had bound them to Him by His own life-blood shed for them.

Not that Kenneth spoke or thought of their design as anything approaching to a martyrdom. Seriously, but joyously, he looked forward to the new life, the new exercise of every faculty in encounters with old rooted superstitions, and the tangled growth of Oriental misbeliefs and disbeliefs, expecting to recognize, under the gorgeous heathen disguises, many an old foe, and trusting to rescue many a brother in arms from conflicts not unlike his own.

The poetry which lay deep in Annie's gentle heart sprang to the light in many sunny dreams of Eastern life and scenery, and perils by sea and land, and the true Enlish home they two would make for each other through it all. With these plans and earnest purposes, there was not a common thing in nature, nor an event in history, nor a philosophical opinion, which Kenneth did not regard with a new interest, and link in some way with his future work. And, added to these, were dearer hopes of gathering many from amidst that hollow heathen society, from barren asceticism, and the worse evils which are its alternate crops, into Christian homes, such as his and Annie's would be, and reclaiming the dead heart to humanity at the same time that he led back the lost soul to God.

They read the Bible diligently, seeking it

as the Father's voice in every difficulty and doubt,—sitting at the feet of the Master like Mary, and drinking in His words. And they found in it not only the sunshine and the guide of their daily path, but the absorbing revelation of the various relationships of God to man, and the mirror in which, to the eye of faith, is traced the marvelous history of the future. Kenneth's soul, at rest as to its own destinies, accepting pardon and peace fully as they were purchased for him, and freely as they were offered to him, was free and at leisure to listen reverently to all God's purposes concerning the future destinies of man, in that Book so wondrously sketched and suggested; thoughts and purposes before which the party strifes and distinctions of to-day shrink into the childish things they are, and nothing seems great but love, and the services it hallows and inspires, —all which flows from God and tends to Him.

The resurrection of the Church and the

deliverance of the earth, the recall of that ancient Royal Nation, forsaken but unforgotten, all centering in the manifestation and visible triumph of Him for whom, when last He came, earth had no resting-place but a grave, and "His own" no welcome but a cross,—these things, studied not in hurry and excitement, but with the calm lowliness of prayer, made the Bible the most glorious sphere for the mind, as well as the dearest and most familiar voice for the heart.

"What a mistake it is," he said one day to Annie, "to look on the Bible as a mere collection of many books! It is so essentially One Book, the first page linked to the last, not by similarity of opinion, but by identity of authorship. Think of those four unobtrusive verses in Genesis relating to Melchizedec, about a thousand years afterwards shining out again as a mysterious type in one of David's Psalms; and a thousand years after that again unfolded by St. Paul into the fullest picture given us of the mediation of Jesus, sacrificing to God for us, blessing us from God, the Priest and King. It is one great, wonderful poem, by One whose ideas are all eternal realities. The simplicity of the old classics is strained and artificial beside its stories and pictures; the vivid visions of Dante are faint and dusky as the air of his Inferno beside its wondrous revelations. And there is this infinite difference between it and all human compositions, its heroes are those who were alive and are dead, and yet are alive for evermore; its visions are not guesses, but glimpses at realities which shall soon familiarly surround us; its thoughts are messages, to each soul among us, from the Lord our God."

XXII.

NEW VISTAS.

WINTER passed, and spring, and summer came again with its fullness of life, but Kenneth's health and Annie's hopes had made no progress, and a cold shadow lay, for her, on all the light. They were all at home again, and Kenneth and Annie were walking in the Eastwood kitchen garden; summer was around them, with its wealth of fulfilled hopes; flowers, not welcomed as they opened one by one, like the earlier ones, "but thronging into life in countless multitude," Kenneth said, "as the holy dead will in the morning when God awakes them;" bees humming busily, yet half-bewildered by the treasures of sweets around them; butterflies and bright-winged insects hovering everywhere in the delicious hush of the summer noon.

"We talk so much of progress, Annie," he said, "yet the law of nature seems to be not growth but change, revolution, not aspiration. The growth of natural things is simple metamorphosis, or successive changes of form, of which decay and death are stages. The dead flower is not glorified into a higher life; it becomes the seed or the food of future generations made in its own image. The burnt coal is not spiritualized into a nobler essence; it is simply dissolved into ashes and gas."

The words dropped coldly on her heart—she said, "But it is not so with us, Kenneth; all this outward growth may be merely apparent, but it is a beautiful type, and we are the reality."

"Yes," he replied, "Nature herself seems full of such things, typifying in one order of beings what she actually develops in another, as the threads of the moss become the stamina of the flower. Yes, Annie, we are the reality, and nature only the shadow. Man is indeed the king and crown of this lower creation;—'the second Man is the Lord from heaven,' and we are His body."

"I sometimes think," he added, after a pause, "we shall never love that grand Oriental scenery as we do this of England. Everything must be so sudden and glowing and startling there, in comparison with the gentle beauty and quiet growth of all around us here. However, we are not to be mere spectators and artists just now, but servants and workers; and in what a work—fellow-workers with God!"

They sat silent for some moments, and then Kenneth resumed abruptly, "What do you think, Annie, of having our missionary station in St. Giles' or Manchester, instead of Hindostan—among the savages of over-civilization? Will you consent to be an exile at home in one of our overgrown cities?"

"It would not be exile, Kenneth, we should

be together—and you know we are to be *strangers* every where."

He drew her arm within his, and they returned to the house.

Gradually the Oriental studies grew more fatiguing—he spoke less and less of those nearer hopes of usefulness, and more of the further hopes, which might, after all, prove the nearest. At first Annie could not bear this change, and endeavored to cheer him by speaking confidently of their future labors. But one day he said,

"Annie, do you think of heaven as a place of rest?"

"A place of rest and praise," she answered.

"I think of it oftenest," he said, "as a place of perfect and joyful work and service. The rest is only for the interval. When once His voice awakes us in the 'hour that cometh,' we shall not need sleep again."

"Yet it is only here, Kenneth, that we can minister to Him 'sick and in prison.'"

"True," he replied gravely, "it is only on earth we can toil and suffer for Him. But for those to whom that may not be given, it is joyful to think that is not the only place for the service of thanksgiving."

The tears filled her eyes as she turned them half-reproachfully on him, and he changed the subject.

But Annie was accustomed to look at things truthfully, and in the evening, when she thought over these words of Kenneth, all her old fears revived; he evidently shared them now. She had heard that in some diseases, the worst symptom was the patient's pertinacious hopefulness. Kenneth's apprehensions, however, were no nervous dread, but a calm and deliberate anticipation. She remembered the opinions of the physician;—the eagerness with which they had construed anything beneath the assurance of the worst into the promise of the best;—how remedy after remedy, from which they had hoped everything, had effected nothing;—

and gradually she fell from that height of unreal hopes on which she had been buoying herself, and saw before her, as a near reality, the possibility from the shadow of which she had fled. She had thought of death as the angel who bears the elect to their rest with God, as an end and a beginning through which we must all one day pass—but as stepping now into the midst of the security of the home circle she had never dreamt of him. For the first time she met the terrible shadow and faced it, and felt that it was indeed no transparent vision through which she could see the light, but a most substantial and irresistible power—it seemed at first the only real power in the world, "the last enemy that shall be destroyed."

Yet she knew, although not destroyed, One had subdued him and commanded him still;—could it then be, that He, the gracious and compassionate Saviour, had given this right to the enemy? For a time, in her anguish, it seemed as if even He—even God her Father — were *against* her, and she pleaded with Him as a helpless captive might for the life of a companion in revolt. She pleaded His mercy and their impotence, and all the purposes they had of love and service in the future; she pleaded the pardon He had given, and should it be limited with such a reservation? His own hand had united them, and could it separate them now? Surely He would not withdraw His own gift, or repent of His own compassion? But as she thus poured forth her sorrow, and pleaded, and remonstrated, and deprecated rather than prayed, a voice came whispering over the depths of her troubled heart, "Dost thou not know me?—it is no spirit—it is no enemy—it is I—be not afraid;" and she listened and became the submissive child once more, and her soul arose in real prayer.

She believed and felt once more that God was *with* her, not sending this trial but *bringing* it to her, and she bowed her soul to receive and welcome Him.

Through all the struggles of that long night, this faith never left her again; and though at times the darkness seemed utter, and the desolation more than she could bear, and all things seemed falling away from her, she knew she was not sinking through an unfathomable void. Underneath her were the everlasting arms.

The summer morning slowly dawned, and she lay down and composed herself for a few hours to rest; but the contrast between the repose of body and the restlessness of heart was more than she could bear; and after lying still one weary hour, she rose, bathed her burning face, dressed, threw open her window, and seated herself at it to read. The song of the early birds, and the dewy freshness of everything, overpowered her; and closing the book, and offering a brief but childlike morning prayer, she went down-stairs and found her work. The mechanical occupation soothed her, and although the tears often blinded her eyes, her thoughts began to flow again in their natural channels of active love and consideration for others.

Kenneth had, perhaps, suspected this long, and had been trying to prepare her for it. She recalled sign after sign which convinced her that it was so. The conversation in the garden, his gradual relinquishing of the studies so ardently commenced, his reluctance to dwell on their future schemes of usefulness; his turning from the deeper and grander parts of the Bible, the histories of past and future ages, to the Psalms, and more direct communings with God, the Epistles, with their treasure of truths and affectionate individual greetings, and the simple narratives of the human life and expiatory death of Jesus. She saw the meaning of it all now, and she had purposely misunderstood him, baffled all his efforts, and refused to enter with him on a subject on which he had sought her sympathy. She resolved it should not be so any longer; and praying for strength, and revived by her affectionate purpose, she met the family at Eastwood with more real cheerfulness than she would have deemed possible a few hours before.

When next Kenneth asked her to read the Bible with him, she commenced the Thessalonians. They read verse by verse; and when he uttered the words—"The dead in Christ shall rise first,"—the thrilling fervor of his voice overcame her, and she could not get beyond the "we which are alive and remain," which followed. Her voice failed, and he read gently on,—

"Shall be caught up together with them in the clouds, and so shall we be ever with the Lord." "It will be no more 'we' and 'they' Annie," he said, "it is, '*together*' again, and '*we*' once more for ever."

The barrier was broken down between them. She wept, but did not try to contradict or check him, and they "comforted one another with these words."

After that they spoke often of death; and

the resurrection, and the rest and the glory which shall follow, took the place of those missionary plans on which they had so loved to dwell.

At first her only hope was of early death and re-union with him in rest, but he pointed out so many who needed her, and showed her how full of blessings and usefulness her life might be, and dwelt so much on the blessedness of being left below to render those services of self-denying love for which all the successive eras of eternity promise no second occasion, that she learned from him to be content to live, if such was their Father's will, as he was content to die.

"It will be very blessed," she said one evening, "for that generation which shall enter together into rest. To them the beginning of rest and glory will be one."

"It will, indeed," he replied. "It is remarkable how little is said in the Bible either regarding the visible world, or the invisible, during that long interval of expectation in which we live, between the rejection of the Lord and His re-appearing. It seems a 'rest,' or parenthesis in the world's history, prolonged in long-suffering grace from year to year,—until the times of the Gentiles are fulfilled. The creation is waiting, the Church on earth is waiting in trial, the saints who have fallen asleep are waiting at rest,—and that is all we know. With His appearing the pause ceases, and the whole chorus of prophecy bursts forth again in songs of triumph. The Psalms, the Prophets, the Apocalypse, are full of that New Song. O Annie, and we shall sing it together!"

"Why," he asked Kate one day, "do you and Gerard never speak of your plans before me? I wish to know and enter into them all." Kate could scarcely reply, "We have no plans, dear Kenneth, until you are well."

He took her hand, and said,

"I may watch the blossom, Kate, though

God call me away before it is opened. Let me think of what and where you will be. 'I asked of Thee life, and Thou gavest me a long life, even forever and ever.'" Kate could not bear to hear him speak so, and left the room; but from that time they began to acknowledge the truth,—the mother last of all.

He loved more than anything to hear them read the narratives in the Gospels,—such a strange vividness and power was given to them by the approach of death.

"They have slept and waited long," he said, "the twice dead, the son of the widow of Nain, and Lazarus, and Jairus's daughter, and the women who ministered to Him, and the apostles, but it cannot seem long with Jesus."

And again, "It is grand and ennobling to enter into what is revealed of God's future purposes concerning our race on earth, but the heavenly Jerusalem is higher and better still. The first truths are the last, the most familiar words are the deepest. The Father's house is better than the thrones of judgment."

And again, "The future is indeed blessed, —but the *nows* of the Bible, how precious they are!—'There is therefore now no condemnation.' 'Beloved, *now* are we the sons of God.'"

He had a class of young men, chiefly from his father's manufactory, and taught them from the Scriptures every Sunday; and when, one Sunday evening, he said, "I shall not be able to take those lads again," they knew the end was near.

"My great sorrow, Annie," he said that same evening, "is that I have done so little, so really nothing for my Saviour. I know He has loved me, and washed me from my sins in His own blood, and I shall appear before Him clothed in His righteousness—but empty-handed, without an offering of gratitude."

"We do not keep our offerings in our own hands," Annie replied, commanding her voice for his sake. "He keeps them, and does not lose or forget the least. And do you think He has taught us nothing through your patience and faith?"

"It is a happy thought that it may be so," he answered; and after a pause, he added fervently, "Yes, even in dying we may bear witness to Him and glorify Him. Pray that this grace may be given to me, Annie."

"Yet," he resumed, "it is a great honor to remain and labor for Him."

"It is far better to depart and be with Him," she murmured.

He took her hand and said tenderly and emphatically,

"Yet for others it was needful that St. Paul should remain, Annie, and he was left. That was better, then, for him. God knew it to be so."

She could not speak, but she smiled

cheerfully through her tears, and they understood each other.

And not long after the far better place was opened to Kenneth, and Annie and all who loved him were left.

XXIII.

NEW VOCATIONS.

THEY were left gazing into heaven after him—until God sent one after another of the manifold claims of everyday life as His messengers to call them from vain and wistful following;—and they went to their active and quiet ministrations of love in their own homes.

At first it was very difficult to Annie above all to look on this death as not indeed an ending of her life and blighting of all hope and purpose—but only a change and beginning of another scene of life.—But she was necessary to many. Her little brothers had a thousand old claims urged with all the peremptoriness of childhood—and her aunt

Cameron leant on her more than on any one. Then, when the first freshness of the loss and grief had passed—as it did pass in time, at least from every one but the mother and Annie—it was difficult to enter into the new hopes and plans which were formed, and to avoid thinking the buoyancy which came back to Kate, and the hopes of the future, which, though dimmed, was still so bright to her and Gerard, rather hollow and heartless, and to recognize that what had darkened life to her, was for them but the hiding of one star. But gradually her heart, braced by the discipline of daily activity, and fed by the reality of promises believed and prayers answered, recovered its tone; and each word of hope which Kenneth had spoken about her usefulness to those he loved, became a legacy of duties, and gradually, not at once, but only by degrees, a sacred vocation unfolded itself to her. By no enthusiastic inward calling, by no irrevocable vow, but really and distinctly, by the voice of irrevocable circumstances, she felt God had called her to a life separate from the closest ties—a life, although marked by no outward sign or profession, but led in the midst of the homes of others, yet of as real and complete self-consecration as any Sister of Charity whose sacrifices and self-denying labors ever made a false religion seem beautiful. She said something of this conviction to Grannie, and Grannie smiled and replied,

"It may be so, my child,—God may make nuns, although we cannot."

It was hard to put off the mourning, the last visible sign of that love which bound her forever to Kenneth. She wished at times they had but been married, that she might have the right to be a mourner for him all her life,—but she rejected the thought as morbid. She was not to have any badge or outward sign to the eyes of men, she was to dress and live and be like all around, and be

> "A creature not too bright or good
> For human nature's daily food,
> For transient sorrows, simple wiles,
> Praise, blame, love, kisses, tears, and smiles,"

that that blessed purpose might not be tarnished by ostentation, or the gaze and remarks of others. And she would not for the world seem sullenly to refuse any measure of joy and consolation which it pleased God to mingle in her cup. She desired, indeed, to be simply and undividedly His servant, but she remembered that above all she was His child; and therefore it was with no feigned cheerfulness and interest that she entered into the preparations for Kate's wedding, and added to them by many little inexpensive conveniences and comforts of which no one else dreamed. She did not seek to keep her heart at any uniform level of stoical endurance—when she was alone manufacturing little things for Kate's wardrobe, she often had to leave her work and weep, and sometimes even when they were together,—but often she joined truly and heartily in every little hope and plan, and felt really refreshed by what she had indeed often entered on with painful effort.

So Kate was married, and the evening had arrived for her return to her bright new home.

They were all there to welcome her, and all had had some share in the preparations, —and for Annie also there was a sweet surprise, as Kate, after mysterious whispers with Mrs. Müller, unlocked a little room over the porch, which Annie had not yet entered, and revealed the very picture of a little bedroom, with writing-table, and sofa, and two cozy chairs, and books, and flowers, and a facsimile of Annie's own white bed, and said, "Dear Annie, this is always yours."

And that evening, as she entered to rest, Annie felt that for her also life had yet fresh flowers.

XXIV.

NEW CARES AND JOYS.

THE coast is left at last, and our little fleet is on the high-seas; henceforth our history must cease to be a narrative, and be limited to an occasional extract from the log-book, as some day of unusual calm or unusual storm is noted—or some green island is touched at for fresh stores—or some vessel hailed with tidings from the old home or the new world.

It was in Kate's home, which has become home-like since we last were there, with a thousand associations—testifying by the presence of sundry economical druggets and coverings, and the absence of sundry delicate ornaments, of the accession of certain disturbing forces in Kate's world. Kate was soberly introducing a miniature frock to its second metempsychosis. Annie Fielding entered through the open window, and seated herself on the nearest chair, to recover her breath after a chase from one of Kate's three little girls, for Annie had the faculty of *playing in earnest* with children, not *playing at play*, that species of complaisance which children so easily see through. Her color was raised with the exertion, so that years might seem to have made even less change than they had in the sweet calm face, which had been grave in childhood, and was childlike in its simple transparent expression now.

The children soon followed, entreating for more play, and joined by four of Jean's boys, who were spending the day with their cousins, until Kate authoritatively interfered, and the petitioners vanished again to the garden, except one quiet little girl, the smallest of the band, who was rather bewildered by the noise of the others, and taking refuge on "cousin Annie's" lap, commenced re-arranging her hair.

"It is very strange," said Kate, "that Jean's children should be so riotous—who would ever have believed, Annie, that she would have borne so composedly the frolics of six noisy boys?"

"I suppose it was what she needed," said Annie, laughing quietly, "we are often educated by contrasts, are we not?—as one of the old Nurnberg sculptors taught his pupils by seeming to teach before them a clumsy, impracticable peasant."

Kate pursued the suggestion inwardly as she proceeded with her cutting-out—"As I am educated to lowly patience by these little cares, and you, sweet, dependent Annie, are disciplined to strength by the loss of that on which you rested." And she looked up and said,

"Maggie, do not tease cousin Annie."

"Cousin Annie is never teased," said the little girl, demurely.

"That is no fault of yours, certainly," replied her mother, laughing.

Just then the other children came in and whispered a low petition to Annie, who was on the point of rejoining them in the garden, when Kate interfered with a maternal veto, and Annie having compounded for a story, the little group were soon at her feet, and the exhaustless petitions for more were at length concluded by the announcement of the nursery dinner.

"How little, Annie, we comprehended of old," said Kate, as they were at length left alone, "what was involved in a holiday."

Annie laughed, but to Kate the question seemed a serious one. Annie had brought with her a book of scriptural interpretation which had interested her very deeply, and had thought this a favorable opportunity of introducing it to Kate.

"I should like it of all things," was the reply, "but I am so busy just now, I am afraid I could not attend to it."

Annie quietly took up her work.

"I think," pursued Kate, after a few minutes, "this will make a most successful best frock for Maggie, which is certainly a brilliant achievement in art, considering all it has gone through; there is certainly an immense pleasure in making a new thing out of an old one. It is quite poetical, if not heroic, to defeat nature and time in this way."

And so the conversation glided off into the small rills of domestic economy, and left Annie's book in the far distance, until a ring at the bell tolled the knell of the leisure hour, and Kate said apologetically, "How provoking, Annie! I was just going to propose reading."—But no one thought the interruption provoking when it was found to proceed from the arrival of Grannie's donkey-chair, and the old lady was greeted with the old fresh welcome, and a general invasion from the nursery. She seemed as great a favorite as "cousin Annie," but an unconscious reverence was mixed with the children's greetings of her, and a thousand silent officious attentions were lavished on her, all lovingly acknowledged, whether needed or not.

Between Annie and her the relation seemed inexpressibly tender. The old lady stroked her hair like a child's as she knelt down beside her, and said,

"You are not a day older, Annie, for this six years' absence—have you made a private compact with time?"

But tears started to Annie's eyes, for she felt she could not return the compliment, and she said cheerfully,

"Yet we *are* traveling onward, dear Grannie."

"Yes—yes, my child, thank God."

"O, Kate," said Annie that evening, as Kate came into her room, the little room over the porch, for a good night, "Grannie is getting old;" and tears silently ran over her cheeks.

Kate seated herself, disposed at first to repel the assertion as a calumny, but as one little sign of weakness after another came to her mind—the occasional weariness with the children, the acceptance of easy chairs and cosy corners, and finally the resignation to the donkey-chair—the truth forced itself on her, and she said nothing.

"I have been thinking," said Annie, "now that my brother George has a curacy, and Elinor is old enough to take my place at home, they might spare me a little, and I might live with Grannie, if she liked. I cannot bear to think of her being left alone with poor old Betsy—she was getting very cross and confused when I left."

Kate caught eagerly at the idea, and in a few days it was all arranged.

The time of Annie's visit to Kate was rapidly wearing away, and the book had never yet found a spare corner of time, although with Gerard she had had much earnest conversation. There were so many things to be discussed: Kate had educational theories to develop and illustrate and compare with Jean's—and theories of domestic economy and costume; and Annie entered into everything so heartily, although she occasionally longed to enter on subjects of higher and broader interest; for the discussions, although frequently starting from some important religious principle, were very apt to be lost in an ocean of small illustrations from Kate's Domestic Chronicles.

"Annie," said Kate one morning, when her cousin's attention had been rather wandering, "how far you are from the petty cares which so bewilder and distract me at times! You bear up navies of good works as if they were flights of poetic swans, whilst I make a great fuss and commotion in turning my mill-wheels. It is not the storm which breaks the image of heaven in the stream, but the million pebbles over which it chafes."

Annie looked up with that gentle sadness which was the nearest approach she ever made to rebuke, and round at the bright room, and the garden, where the children were playing, and down at the fair child asleep on her mother's knee, and said softly,

"Dear Kate, do not call your blessings hindrances."

Kate stretched out her hand and pressed Annie's, and continued,

"I have no hindrances, Annie, but what I make myself, but I am afraid I have acquired some skill in that branch of industry; cares which seemed simple faithlessness for myself, seem necessary for the children, when I think how I can guide them from the shoals where I lost some treasures, and the long future of their lives opens before me—to say nothing of the weakness of seeing patterns of children's dresses and housewifely arrangement, where I used to look for thoughts, opinions, and traits of character."

"Yet your cares are all cleared away like broken toys, when Gerard comes," said Annie.

"Yes, he lives in a purer atmosphere than I," said Kate thoughtfully.

"Is there no Presence always with you, dear Kate, which is the very atmosphere and breath of life, no One always at hand; on whom to unburden cares? Why not cast off your cares, one by one, the moment when, from necessary cares, they become anxieties, instead of walking about with your hands full, and only periodically unloading? O, Kate, do not miss learning the blessed parables God himself would perpetually teach you in your children, and turn the rich blessings He drops into your hand, to bind you to Him, into fetters, by taking the last link out of His hand. Do not turn the most blessed office of woman into a drudgery, by forgetting that you are called to it of God."

Kate made little answer then, but the next day she came early to Annie with her Bible in her hand, and they read and prayed together as of old. And that day many parables were opened to Kate as she watched her children and welcomed her husband. The common-places of her daily life shone with heavenly meaning.

"It was not only in their trustfulness and uncarefulness," she said, "our Lord exhorted us to become as little children, but in their beautiful single-hearted earnestness."

So Annie gave and received, and her gifts enriched herself as much as those that received them. Many cobwebs had been brushed away during her visit—for cobwebs can darken our rooms as well as clouds—and the sunshine came straight into them again from the Sun.

Thenceforward Annie took up her abode with Grannie, having a little bed in the same room.

And many rejoiced in having some share in brightening Grannie's last days—but only Annie was with her when she died.

XXV.

THE NEW HOME.

ONE more glimpse further on. Kate was standing in a small house in a street in Milbourne, in the midst of packages half unpacked. Pecuniary losses had followed one on another in close succession during the last year or two, and had rendered it necessary for both partners to reduce their expenses considerably, so that Gerard had deemed it prudent to remove into the town.

They were now in all the confusion of removing. Kate stood in the midst of the disordered house wearied and dispirited. Things would not fit—curtains were too short for the narrow high windows; carpets were of the wrong shape; everything would betray by a kind of uneasy air that it had known better days. Furniture which had looked fresh and pretty in the bright country-house, seemed dingy and faded in these rooms. Annie came in from the other room with one of the children. "Only come here, mamma, and see how cosy we have made the school-room." Kate followed, but as she looked out on the narrow piece of garden bordered by pent-houses from whose caves the rain was dripping dismally, the words of encouragement well-nigh died on her lips. The little girl was called just then by a joyous little voice ringing through the uncarpeted rooms up-stairs, and ran away, and Kate made no further effort to conceal her depression.

"It begins to look more homelike now, dear Kate," said Annie cheerily.

"It begins to look inhabitable, Annie, but it will never be a home. I used to think money nothing in the treasury of happiness, but it means a great many things. If it were only myself I would not care, but just as the children are getting old enough to appreciate natural beauty it is rather trying. I had so set my heart on their growing up used to every whisper and smile of Nature, and now they will only be her visitors, and see her beauties as sights, not as friends; and what will they do on rainy days? No one can have any idea how trying it is."

She looked up and saw her husband at the door. Her expression and voice changed in a moment as she went to meet him, and Annie, feeling she was not needed, stole up to the children.

Kate began to speak cheerfully to him about the children's plans and busy little arrangements, and turned the bright side of all her own schemes and distresses outward, but he did not seem to heed her. He said nothing, but laid his arm quietly on her shoulder. At length she looked up, and met his eyes fixed on her with an expression of sorrowful tenderness.

"Why do you treat me like one of the

children, Kate?" he said, smiling; "do I not know what a trial this is to you?"

The mask fell off,—her lip quivered, and she hid her weeping face on his arm. He held her silently until the burst of tears was over, and she looked up, and said,

"It is only for the children, Gerard; I did want them to grow up among fields and woods. It is very rebellious of me."

"Have you forgotten the corner of your old kitchen garden at Eastwood, Kate? This square of walled garden may be an Eden to the children yet. And if it is a loss, has not God appointed it, and will not He bring blessing out of it? We have only to help our children to read the lessons of life;—another hand writes them."

"Yes, that is true," she replied. But her bright look was shaded again, and the slow large tears still fell. He said nothing, but kept her hands in his.

"Gerard," she said at length, "what grieves me most in all this is *my grief*. When

Kenneth died, it seemed as if nothing could ever distract my affections again from the heavens which had become his home;—and now that the hand of God has hidden them, from what low things much of the light of my life seems to have flowed! Not from the sky, or even from the fire-side, Gerard, but from the most miserable lucifer-matches,—from walls, and tables, and chairs, and flower-beds, and shrubberies,—the mere externals of my home. The very tassels of our tent, Gerard, are what I have set my heart on. I have worshiped not you, nor the children, nor any beautiful idol of the heart, but mammon, base mammon," she exclaimed, looking up into his eyes with an expression of mingled disgust and penitence.

"The serpent is detected then," he said, "and the end is gained; is it not?"

"It is not a serpent, but a toad, which has been squatting at the ear of Eve," she replied, smiling, and brushing away her tears as if she would brush away all murmurs with them forever. "I did not feel it at first, Gerard," she continued gravely; "when first you told me of our losses, they seemed nothing; the words of hope and contentment I spoke to you were not feigned; I felt quite heroic. I had you and the children—was I not still rich? But gradually, as one thing after another had to be parted with, and all the uncomfortable details pressed on me, my heart sank,—and I felt out of place—and *wronged*, Gerard."

"God would not have His chastenings seem nothing," he replied very tenderly; "He would have them felt."

"But O, Gerard, I have not only mourned, I have murmured."

"*We* have sinned, Kate," he said gravely, "but *He loves us*—there is forgiveness with Him—and we have Jesus."

And that evening their prayer together had a new fervor and freshness, chiefly, perhaps, because they had learned that day something more of the need of the meaning of the name of Jesus. Thus they were truly helpers of one another's joy.

"If we walk in the light, as He is in the light, we have fellowship one with another; —and," that the soiled feet may be purified to walk in that path of blessing, "the blood of Jesus Christ cleanseth from all sin."

The next day Gerard brought in a letter to Kate. She took it from his hand and read,

"MY DEAR KATE,—Your uncle and I have been thinking your children might miss their country play-grounds, and like to play in the Vicarage gardens. Your garden opens on the passage leading to the Glebe Fields. If you like to have a door made in your walls, we will send you the key of our gate, and you can use it whenever you please.—Your affectionate aunt,

AUGUSTA FIELDING.

"N.B. Allow me to ask you to desire the children not to gather the flowers, and to lock the gate always after them."

Kate gave the note back, and said between laughing and crying, "Dear aunt Fielding! that is real self-denial in her, to introduce such mischievous elves among her neat borders. There is one fruit of our trial, Gerard," she added, with one of her brightest smiles, "we may be lesson-books for others also."

And when the day came for them to migrate finally into the new house, and the three children met them at the door, and insisted on doing the hospitalities, escorting their mother upstairs, and ensconcing her in an easy chair by a table on which stood a nosegay from the new garden, Kate looked up to Gerard and said,

"Is it not like a second honey-moon, Gerard?"

"With just a little plainer writing from the hand of God on the walls, to remind us that it is not our Father's house," he replied quietly.

XXVI.

THE OLD HOME.

THEY were gathered round the fire at Eastwood a few evenings afterwards, after the early tea.

Mrs. Cameron was there, looking younger than she had for years. The reverse of fortune seemed to have given her new faculties. It had obliged her to do many things herself which she had been accustomed to depute to others, and the exercise had strengthened and braced her whole nature, and made her discover and rejoice in many additional means of usefulness. She was explaining a picture-book to Maggie.

Mr. Cameron looked more aged than any one, yet the deep lines on his face relaxed from the furrows of care into gentle footprints of time and thought, as he listened to the eager histories of little Catharine and Agnes, and, while they thought him their teacher, learned from their childish lips sweet lessons of Christian faith and hope. Kate and Gerard were engaged in low, serious conversation on the sofa. Annie also was there. It was one of those gatherings which tempted her to feel a little lonely. Every one had some one nearer and dearer to them than she could ever be, and the thought of Kenneth and of Grannie was on her heart. But more and more that thought had grown from a regret into a hope. And looking at the fire, she mused—

"Who would have dreamed when the old trees withered and fell one by one in the primeval forest, until it sank into a dismal swamp, that God was preparing them thus to be the light and comfort of our fireside to-night? We may well trust His hand to prepare."

And she looked upwards and prayed for a

blessing on all around, and was at peace again—and in spirit she filled up the vacant places in the circle, and looked forward to that day when the whole family in earth and heaven shall be gathered in the presence of Him of whom it is named. Yet when she retired to her own room in the old Vicarage, something of the feeling of loneliness and sadness came over her again. There was the old furniture a little faded, the old books a little worn, and her own face, as she caught its reflection in the glass, middle-aged and faded too. Much had passed away from her, and so little fresh seemed to have sprung up instead! She thought of Kate's life, with its full swelling tide of blessings, and her own seemed stagnant beside it. She opened her large old-fashioned desk, mechanically, —but as one letter after another caught her eye, it brightened into its usual calm cheerfulness again, a cheerfulness which in itself gave light.

There were family letters of all sorts and

sizes,—grievances, joys, cares, perplexities, from the school-boy's to the man's, from one nursery era to another, poured out into Annie's heart; and beyond this inner circle, many others as precious in their way. There was the old fashioned cramped hand of an old maiden lady, whom she had awakened from a supreme interest in her own preservation to an interest in the orphaned, and sick, and poor in her neighborhood,—there were the unformed hands of children, who owed their first impressions of the love of God to her,—there were scrawls from Sunday scholars, twenty grateful words filling a sheet—there were thickly crossed epistles from governesses in families she had visited, to whom her friendship was the sunshine of many weary and apparently fruitless labors, —there were foreign letters from emigrants who had found new homes in the New World, and from Missionary Stations, to which her budgets of home news and sympathy were like angels' messages. Her desk was her fireside. And as she sat there and looked at these and at the miniatures of Kenneth and Grannie which lay among them, and thought of the many messages of love and comfort which had been committed to her, and of the joy and the meetings which were in store; and, above all, of that one meeting with Him to whom she owed all; her eyes filled with tears, and she said, in her heart, to Him who can hear and does listen, "How could I ever think myself lonely and poor!"

Kate found, as the months passed on, a thousand blessings in the new sphere. There were children with comfortless homes, and a daily governess without a home, and two little orphan girls at school, to whom a day with her bright family circle was a festival. There were so many little acts of neighborly kindness which distance had rendered impossible before,—there was the relationship with the factory workmen and their families,—there was education for the hearts of her children, richer and deeper than all they could gather from the instrumental music of nature, in sharing the joys and sorrows of those around.

"I have sometimes thought, Annie," she said one evening as they sat in the old seat in the Eastwood kitchen-garden looking over the valley, "that you had more means of entire self-consecration to God than I, but it is not so; all callings give scope for the services of Christian love. The glimmering of the fireside may guide and cheer the wanderer at times, as well as the lamp in the hand of those who come through the snows to search for him. Priscilla and Aquila had their share of self-denying labors and apostolic greetings, as well as Phœbe, servant of the church."

Annie was silent.—Kate looked at her inquiringly.

"I was thinking," Annie said, "what a dream and fairy-tale any one page in our lives would look beside any other ten years distant, and yet how nothing in our lives is a dream, but everything leaves fruits or footprints. I was looking at our island, Kate, and thinking of the evening when dear Grannie went there with us."

The tears started to Kate's eyes, and she said,

"Life seemed like a play-ground then,—and since we have found it is a school-room."

"But we would not go back," Annie replied, with her quiet smile; "the school has its play-ground, and we have time between the lessons for many hymns and songs of thanksgiving, and by-and-by we shall find all our lessons, even the hardest, turned into songs."

"And it is an industrial school, too," rejoined Kate; "there is time for doing as well as learning, and the Master deigns to keep our childish manufactures, and treasure them, Annie."

"He is also our Father," Annie said softly. "But, dear Kate, the happiest thought is, that He himself is remolding us, not only working by us, but working in us, and that by-and-by, like our Lord, we shall please Him perfectly. He does not forget the least service of love which He inspires,—and we have only to remember Him. We are to minister to others for His sake; and O, Kate, how ceaselessly and bountifully He ministers to us!"

Thus Kate and Annie had each their fit discipline, and were each called and trained at the right time, and in the right way, to be Sisters of Mercy and handmaids of the Lord. And Grannie was not left childless.

THE END.

BY A. L. O. E.

The Straight Road the Safest and Surest, .	45
Stories of Jewish History, ...	60
Cortley Hall (containing the above two),	90
Paying Dear, and other Stories, . . .	60
Esther Parsons, and other Stories, . . .	60
Try Again (containing the last two), . .	90
The Three Bags of Gold, ...	60
Falsely Accused, and other Stories,. . .	60
Christian Conquests (containing the last two), .	90
The Silver Casket, or Wiles of the World, .	90
Good for Evil, and other Stories. 6 engr., .	90
Ned Franks and other Stories, . . .	60
The Red Cross Knight, ...	60
The Christian's Panoply, (containing the last two) .	90

"We would rather be 'A. L. O. E.' than Thackeray or Dickens. We have not the least idea who or what the author is, represented by those four letters; but one thing is certain--he (or she, perhaps) is exerting a power far more to be desired than the reputation of the mere novelist, however dazzling that may be.—*C. Times.*

THE DAWN OF HEAVEN. By the late Rev. JOSEPH A. COLLIER, with a brief Biographical Sketch, and a Portrait by Ritchie. $1 50.

From the Biographical Sketch.

"The watchful eyes of those nearest to him could not fail to mark, in his increasing zeal, spirituality and tenderness, that he was rapidly ripening for the inheritance that fadeth not away. The abode of the blessed was real to him and bright before him; pouring from its open gates its glory and its joy down into his soul. This book, The Dawn of Heaven,' is the ripe fruit of these celestial communings, presenting the thoughts of his holiest moments and the hallowed results of his nearest approaches to God."

SEA DRIFTS. By Mrs. G. A. H. MACLEOD. 16mo, illustrated. $1 25

"This is a story of girls' school days, in which Maude, who had been a sea-drift from a wreck, figures as the principal character. She possesses many virtues, and was an example to her companions. She is at length identified by her foreign friends, and this terminates the pleasant story."—*Presbyterian.*

GOD'S WAY OF HOLINESS. By HORATIUS BONAR, D. D.. Author of "Hymns of Faith and Hope." Red edges. Uniform with the "Hymns." $1 50.

"The rich scriptural exhibition of a great subject made in this book, commends it to the study of every believer and unbeliever also. The style is animated, and the illustrations such as a man of a poetical temperament would be likely to employ. Such a book as this is well adapted to promote personal holiness in the church, to quicken Christians in the Divine life, and by the blessing of God it will be greatly useful."—*N. Y. Observer.*

EGYPT'S PRINCES; A Narrative of Missionary Labour in the Valley of the Nile. By the Rev. GULIAN LANSING, American Missionary to Cairo. 12mo. $1 50.

"The author, in his preface, makes a defence of those 'missionaries who are dull and uninteresting in their narratives.' He will not, however, need any such apologist for himself, for with the exception of a few of the earlier chapters, his book is lively without exaggeration, and earnest without partiality. Those interested in the present condition of that marvelous old country watered by the Nile will find "Egypt's Princes" the most intelligent, accessible, and inexpensive of the recent additions to the large list of published works on the land of the Pyramids."—*Evening Post.*

THE CHRONICLES OF A GARDEN. Its Pets and its Pleasures. By the late Miss HENRIETTA WILSON, Author of "Little Things," etc. Printed on fine tinted paper, and beautifully illustrated. Gilt. $2 50.

"This is one of the most beautiful books, both in matter and manner, that we have ever seen."—*N. E. Farmer.*

TALES AND SKETCHES OF CHRISTIAN Life in many Lands and Ages. By the Author of "The Schönberg-Cotta Family." 16mo. $1 25.

(This work can also be had in two 18mo vols. for Sabbath School Libraries, as follows):

Maia and Cleon, - - - 60
Diary of Brother Bartholomew, - 60

"The nameless authoress of 'The Schönberg-Cotta Family' has obtained a reputation which, in degree and kind is reached by few among even noble and familiar names. Any thing from her pen is sure of a welcome, and, more important, is not less sure of deserving it. The present volume contains several sketches based upon chapters of Church history which deserve to be better known."

THE MARTYRS OF SPAIN, AND THE Liberators of Holland. By the same Author. $1 25.

"The author, who has thrown so much fascination over the history of Luther, in the great work of Reformation, has adopted the same plan in illustrating anew the fierce and relentless persecution in Spain against the Protestants. The history of martyrology in that God-forsaken country is skillfully condensed in the first part, while in the second, a careful *resume* is made of the redemption of Holland from Popish domination."—*Presbyterian.*

THE CRIPPLE OF ANTIOCH. By the Author of the "Schönberg-Cotta Family." $1 25.

"These Sketches present vivid pictures of life among the early Christians in the generation immediately following the apostolic days. The first of the three is mainly an imaginative story, a tale of a crippled Greek girl a convert to Paul's preaching at Antioch; but it is a story beautifully told, and full of the spirit of that earnest time, when the utter novelty of Christian truth gave it marvelous freshness and power."—*Springfield Republican.*

THE TWO VOCATIONS. By the same Author. 16mo. $1.25

ST. PAUL THE APOSTLE. A Biblical Portrait and Mirror of the Manifold Grace of God. By W. F. BESSER, D. D. With an Introductory Notice by Dr. HOWSEN. $1 50.

THE FORTY DAYS AFTER OUR LORD'S Resurrection. By the Rev. WM. HANNA, LL. D. 12mo. $1 50.

NED'S MOTTO; or, Little by Little. By the Author of "Win and Wear," "Faithful and True," and "Tony Starr's Legacy." 16mo. $1 25.

"A simple story, but a good one, of a lad orphaned by this war, who works his way on by short steps, but sure, to the possession of a worthy character and the enjoyments of its benefits."—*Boston Recorder.*

MABEL'S EXPERIENCE; or, Seeking and Finding. 18mo. 90c.

THE FOOT OF THE CROSS. By the Rev. OCTAVIUS WINSLOW. 18mo. 90c.

THE POST OF HONOR. By the Author of "Broad Shadows on Life's Pathway." 16mo $1 25.

"A pleasant little story. It contains scenes of genuine pathos and earnest struggle. The groundwork of the story is the Madagascar Persecution, interwoven with which are many very interesting scenes."

THE PROPHET OF FIRE (Elijah). By the Rev. J. R. MACDUFF, D. D. 12mo. $1 50.

"The theme is well suited to Dr. Macduff's bold style of discourse and to his warm-hearted Christian glow. Elijah was a hero as well as a righteous man, and his history is full of dramatic action and fire."—*Boston Recorder.*

ELLEN MONTGOMERY'S BOOKSHELF. By the Author of the "Wide, Wide World," and "Dollars and Cents." 5 vols. in a neat box. $6 00.

"Ellen Montgomery's Bookshelf" is a perfect treasure of good things for juvenile readers. The estimable and experienced writers well know how to interweave the highest lessons of truth and duty with the simplest language and the most agreeable narratives."—*American Presbyterian.*

The Volumes are sold separately, and are as follows:

1. Mr. Rutherford's Children, . . . 1 20
2. Sybil and Chryssa; a Sequel to the above, 1 20
3. Hard Maple, ... 1 20
4. Carl Krinken, His Christmas Stocking, . 1 20
5. Casper and His Friends, . . . 1 20

THE BOOK OF ANIMALS, or THE WONDERS of the Menagerie. Profusely illustrated. 90c.

THE CHILD'S BUNYAN. 18mo, . . 60

GASCOYNE, OR THE SANDAL WOOD Trader. A Tale of the Pacific. By R. W. BALLANTYNE. Coloured Plates. 16mo. $2 00.

THE WORKS OF PRESIDENT EDWARDS. 4 vols. 8vo, cloth. $12 00. . . . .

This edition of the works of the greatest American Theologian was formerly published by Leavitt & Allen. We have bought the stereotype plates and all the printed copies.

www.ingramcontent.com/pod-product-compliance
Lightning Source LLC
LaVergne TN
LVHW010156110826
845151LV00002B/535

* 9 7 8 1 4 2 5 5 3 7 0 6 7 *